Praise for the Inspector DeKok Investigates series by Baantjer

"Along with such peers as Ed McBain and Georges Simenon, [Baantjer] has created a long-running and uniformly engaging police series. They are smart, suspenseful, and better-crafted than most in the field."
—*Mystery Scene*

"Baantjer's laconic, rapid-fire storytelling has spun out a surprisingly complex web of mysteries."
—*Kirkus Reviews*

"DeKok is a careful, compassionate policeman in the tradition of Maigret; crime fans will enjoy this book."
—*Library Journal*

"DeKok's maverick personality certainly makes him a compassionate judge of other outsiders and an astute analyst of antisocial behavior."
—*The New York Times Book Review*

"It's easy to understand the appeal of Amsterdam police detective DeKok; he hides his intelligence behind a phlegmatic demeanor, like an old dog that lazes by the fireplace and only shows his teeth when the house is threatened."
—*The Los Angeles Times*

Inspector DeKok Investigates

Titles Available or Forthcoming from Speck Press

DeKok and
the Dead Harlequin

by
A. C. Baantjer

Translated by H. G. Smittenaar

speck press
golden

Published by Speck Press
An imprint of Fulcrum Publishing
4690 Table Mountain Drive, Suite 100 • Golden, Colorado 80403
800-992-2908 • 303-277-1623 • speckpress.com

© 2009 Speck Press. Translated from *De Cock en de dode harlekijn* by
Baantjer, © 1978 by Uitgeverij De Fontein. 1st Dutch printing 1967, 1st
American printing 1992.

ISBN: 978-1-933108-27-8

Library of Congress Cataloging-in-Publication Data

Baantjer, A. C.
 [De Cock en de dode harlekijn. English]
 Dekok and the dead harlequin / by A.C. Baantjer ; translated from the
Dutch by H. G. Smittenaar.
  p. cm. -- (Inspector DeKok series ; no. 6)
 ISBN 978-1-933108-27-8 (pbk.)
 I. Smittenaar, H. G. II. Title.
 PT5881.12.A2C56213 2009
 839.31'364--dc22

                                2008031647

10 9 8 7 6 5 4 3 2 1

Book layout and design by Margaret McCullough
Cover image © Shutterstock
Printed in the United States by United Graphics Incorporated

1

The envelope was addressed to Inspector DeKok at the renowned police station on Warmoes Street, located on the edge of Amsterdam's Red Light District.

Inspector DeKok opened it; at first glance the content seemed ridiculous. Or was it? The note was short and written in an easy, fluid handwriting. The writer had a laconic, but lucid, style.

Dear Inspector DeKok:

I have seriously decided to kill a man. For obvious reasons I cannot tell you the name of the intended victim, nor will I tell you the place and the time of the murder. In any case, that has already been decided. There are, however, just a few unimportant details that I would like to discuss with you in advance. Would Wednesday night, eight o'clock exactly, be convenient for you?

Yours Very Truly,

Pierre Brassel

The station house was often described as the busiest police station in Western Europe. DeKok seemed lost in the large, inhospitable detective room on the second floor. His tired, often painful feet rested on the desk. His short, strong fingers raked his gray hair. His broad face, lined with the deep marks of a good-natured boxer, looked solemn. He was not at all happy. He had read the strange note several times. Each time he read it, he was as surprised as he had been the first time.

This was an entirely new wrinkle in a career of more than twenty years. A person contacts Homicide and details in a short, businesslike letter his intention to kill someone. DeKok felt he'd entered the theater of the absurd.

Of course, he could recall plenty of instances in which a murder had been announced in advance. Not this way, however. Usually such announcements were full of self-justification and pathos. They were unfailingly anonymous. But this note, which wasted hardly a word, was signed, presumably with a real name.

DeKok looked up Brassel in the phone book. He dialed the number.

"Hello?"

"Yes."

"Mr. Brassel?"

"Speaking."

"Inspector DeKok, Homicide. I, eh…"

"Oh, yes. You're from Warmoes Street. Inspector DeKok, did you receive my letter?"

"Yes."

"Fine. Is eight o'clock convenient?"

"Yes, that, eh…"

"Fine, fine. Expect me. I shall be on time."

Before DeKok could ask a single question, Brassel broke the connection. DeKok thought it inadvisable to call back right away.

After about half an hour, unable to contain his curiosity, DeKok tried the line again and found it engaged. It remained busy every time he called. Pierre Brassel seemed a busy man.

After a few more failed attempts, DeKok angrily slammed the receiver down. If nothing else, he was comforted that he had asked his partner Vledder to do some digging around. Maybe that would bring some clarity to the circumstances.

To help get his anger under control, he stood in front of the small mirror over the water fountain and uttered a number of unflattering things for about two minutes. He said things about foolish people and how they so often succeeded in plaguing him, DeKok, with near insoluble puzzles.

Finally, he decided not to call anymore. He decided to just wait for the appointment. At least he knew that somewhere in Amsterdam there was a Pierre Brassel who had written him a remarkable little letter.

DeKok stood up. He paced past deserted desks with his typical, somewhat swaying gait and his hands deep in his trouser pockets. He tried to form a picture of Pierre Brassel in his mind, a picture that would fit with the voice he had heard over the telephone. He did not succeed.

He stopped in front of the window and looked outside, slowly rolling back and forth on the balls of his feet. His gaze passed over the backlit rooftops of the houses across the street and rested on the illuminated tower of the Old Church, so called because the New Church was a mere three hundred years old. It was seven thirty. He hoped Vledder would finish soon, in any case before eight.

"Well?"

With an amused smile on his handsome face, Vledder looked at his mentor. "Well, if, eh, you ask me," he said thoughtfully, "then, somebody's trying to play some sort of joke on you."

"A joke?"

"Yes."

DeKok slipped lazily into his chair and looked at the still-boyish face of his congenial partner and pupil.

"If that's the case, my friend," he said with just a tiny hint of sarcasm, "when am I supposed to start laughing? At the time this joker Brassel lets me in on the joke, or when a murder really *has* been committed? Tell me, please."

Vledder pulled a moody face. DeKok's remarks seemed to have offended him.

"But it's crazy," he exclaimed stubbornly. "Totally foolish. I'm sorry, DeKok, but I can't see the seriousness of it." He snorted deprecatingly. "Come on, admit it, who would write such a letter? Even if somebody planned to kill somebody, they certainly wouldn't announce it to the police. Nobody does that."

DeKok looked at him.

"Nobody?"

"Well, maybe somebody who's crazy."

DeKok rubbed his large nose with the back of his hand.

"So you think he's crazy?"

Vledder sighed deeply. "No," he admitted, shaking his head. "No, I don't think Brassel is crazy. That is, during my investigation today, there was no indication of that. On the contrary, the people who discussed him with me generally agreed Pierre Brassel has above-average intelligence."

DeKok nodded.

"That's too bad," he said hesitatingly. "I honestly wonder whether it is something to fear."

"Why?"

DeKok rubbed his chin with the other hand.

"Well, if Pierre Brassel were known as a friendly, harmless madman, everything would be a lot easier. I'd just make one quick phone call to the nut removal team; they could take him away and observe him for a few days. As things stand, though…" He did not complete the sentence, but scratched the back of his neck. "What exactly does our above-average friend do for a living?"

Vledder pulled a chair closer to the desk.

"Brassel and his elderly father own a modest but highly regarded accounting firm, along Emperor's Canal. The business is a holdover from the previous century, an unshakable monument of solid respectability."

DeKok laughed.

"One calls that renowned."

Vledder made a nonchalant gesture.

"Have it your way," he grunted. "A renowned accountant's office, with a bookkeeper, a clerk, and a darling of a secretary."

"Old?"

"Who?"

"The secretary."

"Oh, hardly! She's twenty-three, with chestnut hair, olive skin, and green flashing eyes. She has an irresistible dimple in her left cheek, or, wait a moment, no, it was the right cheek, yes, the right cheek."

DeKok looked searchingly at his younger colleague.

"Apparently you spent some time with the hardly old lady?"

Vledder grinned broadly.

"Yes, with the assumed identity of an inspector of historic preservation coming to look at the interior of the old canal house."

"Did you meet Brassel?"

Vledder shook his head.

"No, I managed to avoid him. When the secretary started to insist she wanted to introduce me, I quickly made my excuses and disappeared." He smiled at the memory. "It's a dank, old office, but the secretary..." He looked dreamily into the distance.

DeKok tapped a finger on the desk.

"What about family?"

"Whose?" Vledder asked absentmindedly.

DeKok jumped up.

"Not the secretary's family!" he said, irritated.

Vledder swallowed. DeKok's heated voice brought him back to reality. He took his notebook from his pocket and read in a monotonous voice.

"Pete or, as he prefers to be called, Pierre Brassel is a handsome man, attractive to women. He's thirty-three. According to my informants, he finished high school and college without any problem. He continued his studies and became a certified public accountant. Immediately upon obtaining his CPA, he was offered a management position in the office. He's been married almost five years, has two children, a boy and a girl. His son is three years old, his daughter is eighteen months. There appears to be no friction in the household. The family lives in a nice villa outside of town, just off the road to Schiphol Airport. There is almost no mortgage left on the house. The financial status of the family is evidently solid."

DeKok grunted.

"An altogether respectable citizen."

Vledder nodded.

"Exactly, a solid citizen. The terms *murderer* or *latent killer* don't spring to mind. I've been unable to discover anything negative about the man. As far as anyone knows, there are no skeletons in his closet. He's not in the police files." He rose from his chair and began to pace up and down the detective room. He halted in front of DeKok's desk. "I don't know what *you* think about it," he said with a gesture of barely suppressed impatience, "but as far as I'm concerned we've already wasted far too much time on that idiotic letter."

Thoughtfully, DeKok chewed his lower lip.

"I hope," he said uncertainly, "you're right. In any case, let's wait for Pierre Brassel. It's only three minutes until eight."

2

DeKok watched the clock like a raptor, barely blinking.

He realized his constant gaze was becoming compulsive. Although he could not explain it, his eyes remained fixed on the clock's second hand. It was like an athletic event in slow motion; it was impossible to resist watching

Driven by the same subconscious compulsion, he had asked Vledder to check the time by telephone; they had then synchronized their watches. DeKok had an intuition. He had the feeling time would be of vital importance. It was of the utmost importance to Pierre Brassel.

A few seconds before eight, the partners heard sounds of footsteps in the corridor leading to the detective room. Within seconds they could see an indistinct shadow against the frosted glass of the door.

Both inspectors looked on silently, Vledder annoyed and DeKok tensely expectant.

The arm of the shadow rose and knocked softly on the glass.

"Enter," called DeKok.

There was a moment of hesitation. Once the door opened, a tall, slender, handsome man entered. He gave a confusing first impression. There was something unbalanced about his appearance. He looked something like a Calvinist church warden out on a weekday. He wore a long, somber dark coat, but the pearl gray scarf he wore outside the collar gave him an elegant, worldly appearance. The most noticeable feature, however, was his high forehead, which was accented by a receding hairline. A mocking grin played around his weak, thin-lipped mouth.

"I have an appointment," he said, carefully enunciating every letter, "an appointment for eight o'clock exactly." He glanced at the electric clock on the wall. "I notice with pleasure that I am exactly on time. My name is Pierre Brassel." He announced himself like a game-show host announcing a new champion.

DeKok looked at him searchingly for several seconds, trying to sort out his impression of the baffling visitor, but the man remained enigmatic. Slowly he extended a hand.

"DeKok," he said vaguely. "DeKok with, eh, a kay-oh-kay." He pointed at his younger partner. "This is Inspector Vledder, my invaluable partner."

Pierre Brassel grinned again, and DeKok offered him a chair next to the desk.

The first skirmishes passed in a calm atmosphere. At first it was no more than a mutual, careful probing. The men exchanged the usual platitudes and banalities, fleshed out with polite clichés. Vledder cracked Pierre Brassel's façade, eliciting the first real emotion. In a casual tone, he said, "Homicide really cannot be bothered with practical-joke letters. The police department is not an institution charged with providing public entertainment." For that, he opined, there were different avenues.

Vledder's remarks hit a sore spot.

Pierre's eyes glistened dangerously. He spread his arms in a theatrical gesture.

"But gentlemen," he exclaimed, irritated and with a hint of astonishment, "surely you have not considered my note a tasteless joke? Really! The very idea is insufferable. In fact, it would be an insult to me, a very grave insult. I am no charlatan."

Vledder grinned broadly.

"Oh no?" he asked mockingly. "Not a charlatan, you say?"

Agitated, Brassel stood up. Vledder's question had visibly upset him. His indignation was not an act, it was real. A red flush colored his cheeks.

"This is the limit," he cried angrily. "I did not come here to be ridiculed. I wrote you about a matter I assumed would be of interest to your department. You agreed to this appointment, to discuss a case. I did everything in accordance with common decency and good manners. There is no reason why you should—"

DeKok raised a hand in a restraining gesture.

"Please sit down and calm yourself, Mr. Brassel," he said soothingly. "I ask your indulgence and I apologize for my young colleague. You must admit it does seem strange for an intelligent man to contact Homicide in order to acquaint us with his intent to commit murder."

Brassel forced his lips into a winning smile.

"Your colleague," he said, much calmer, "is not just young and tactless, he also lacks imagination."

DeKok looked at him, his head cocked to one side.

"How's that?" he asked, interested.

Brassel sighed and resumed his seat.

"How can I best explain it," he said slowly, looking for words. "I'll give you an example: if you intend to plant flowers in your garden and you are not sure about timing or the best method for planting, you will ask for advice from a florist or a gardener. Logical, I should think. After all, they are professionals." He laughed pleasantly and gestured vaguely toward DeKok with a slender hand. "I have taken it upon myself to commit murder, so where do I go for professional help?" He looked smugly about, as if expecting a spontaneous answer from an attentive audience. Then he answered his own question. "Of course, from the famous Inspector DeKok, expert in homicide."

There was a sudden silence.

DeKok looked intently at the gleaming, beaming face of Brassel and tried to detect a hint of the facetious. He saw none. He encountered a pair of cunning, alert eyes that carefully measured the reaction created by the earlier remarks. He got his reaction.

Vledder looked at Brassel with wide, surprised eyes, and DeKok swallowed. It took a while before he trusted himself to speak again.

"I believe," he said heatedly, "you have made a serious mistake. Your comparison is incorrect. Your premise is faulty. I'm not an expert in the committing of murders. I merely try to solve them. I bring perpetrators to justice after they have committed murders. *Others* commit the crimes. You understand?"

Pierre Brassel nodded emphatically and showed rows of white teeth.

"Exactly, yes," he cried enthusiastically. "Exactly right! And that is precisely why I addressed what you think is such a ridiculous letter to you. You have experience with murder. Afterward, you can say exactly what mistakes the killer has made. Why should I not utilize your knowledge to avoid mistakes of my own?"

He moved his chair slightly and sighed deeply. Then he continued. "See here, Inspector," he said earnestly, "you can only start your work after I have committed a crime, not before! That is too late for my purposes. I cannot change my actions once the deed is done, so to speak. From that moment on, you and I have to be enemies. A normal, open exchange of ideas will cease to be possible. Obviously our goals will no longer be mutual. Right now, under the present circumstances, I mean, during the preliminaries, we could..."

He did not complete the sentence. He appeared to ponder something, turning it over in his mind.

"Inspector," he said after a considerable silence, and with a more determined tone of voice, "I want to make you an honest offer. You tell me what mistakes to avoid in committing my murder, and I will deliver myself to you as the culprit." Brassel smiled charmingly. "Call it a gentlemen's agreement," he added.

He paused. When DeKok did not react, he continued, "In fact, you already have my part of the bargain in your hands. I have delivered myself to you. I just have yet to do what I must. You understand? My motive is to commit the perfect crime."

DeKok rubbed his broad face with his hands. He peeked at Brassel from between his fingers. It was as though DeKok hoped the image would vanish. The visitor looked as if he had just spread a royal flush on a poker table.

"I do believe," answered DeKok quietly, "I understand you. You expect from me, as the expert in the field, a set of instructions for the perfect murder. A sort of recipe."

"Indeed."

"A complete recipe, including all the ingredients to guarantee you will not be caught or punished."

Brassel nodded joyfully.

"Exactly!" he said.

DeKok pushed his lower lip forward.

"In exchange, you offer me inside knowledge. I'll know you committed the murder." DeKok's voice dripped with sweet sarcasm. "That's what you mean, right?"

"Indeed, that is what I mean."

"You underestimate me," grinned DeKok. "It seems to me a rather one-sided agreement. It seems I would know you committed a murder but would be unable to prove your guilt, thanks to *my* recipe. No one prosecutes a murderer who has managed to commit the perfect crime. What's in it for me? Nothing! Absolutely nothing. You offer me a perpetrator, but with no ability to serve justice."

Pierre Brassel gave him his most winning smile.

"You are clever, Inspector. You're right, I just want to escape the consequences." He shrugged his shoulders in a negligent gesture. "Understandable, do you not agree? I am relatively young. I have a darling wife and two wonderful children, a good job. It would be too silly to risk all that for a somewhat belated murder." He halted suddenly, smiling sheepishly. For the first time it seemed as if he had lost part of his self-control.

DeKok looked at him, a challenge in his eyes.

"What do you mean, 'somewhat belated'?" he asked.

Brassel stroked his temples with the flat of his hands.

"You *will* find out," he said slowly. "Believe me, you will see. There is no reason to get ahead of ourselves."

A new silence fell upon the room.

Vledder, who leaned against a wall diagonally behind Brassel, pointed at his head with a meaningful look. The gesture did not escape DeKok. He released a deep sigh, again focusing his attention on Brassel.

"You *are*," he asked wearily, "actually planning to commit murder?"

"Yes, I am. Even if you do not help me, even without the help of a foolproof recipe. I wrote it clearly enough. I've already decided upon the time and place. Nothing can change my mind."

DeKok leaned forward and studied Brassel's face with care.

"Seriously," he said finally, "you really didn't expect for a moment I would help you commit murder, now did you?"

Pierre Brassel looked up and shook his head. A sad smile marred his handsome face.

"No," he answered cheerlessly, "I did not believe that for an instant."

DeKok's eyebrows rippled slightly. People who knew the senior inspector swore his eyebrows lived a life of their own. It was certain those eyebrows could do gymnastics outside the capabilities of ordinary eyebrows. Vledder watched with fascination. He thought he could sometimes predict DeKok's actions or words from the way the eyebrows moved. He was always wrong.

"Let's get to why you wrote the letter," said DeKok.

Brassel did not answer. He stretched his left arm slightly forward, pushed the sleeve of his coat back, and looked intently at his watch.

"Why," repeated DeKok, irritated, "did you write me the letter?"

Brassel completely ignored the question. He kept staring at his watch without raising his eyes. After a few seconds he stood up and looked first at DeKok, then at Vledder, then back again. His demeanor changed. He took the spotlight, like a toastmaster ready to begin the long-winded, well-rehearsed introduction of the next speaker.

"Gentlemen," he announced dramatically, "in room twenty-one of the Greenland Arms Hotel, about three hundred yards from here as the crow flies, you will find the corpse of Jan Brets."

"What?"

Pierre Brassel grinned.

"Jan Brets," he continued cheerfully. "His skull is crushed."

He gestured toward the telephone on DeKok's desk.

"Please call them," he encouraged, "the Greenland Arms Hotel, or send one of your alert constables to verify."

DeKok's eyes narrowed dangerously.

"What kind of a joke is this?!" DeKok roared in anger.

Brassel gave him a sad look.

"It seems," he said, shaking his head, "you find it difficult to take me seriously. Am I right?"

DeKok bit his lower lip and stared at the eccentric before him. He could not penetrate the thoughts of his adversary. Neither could he tread the tightrope between joviality and seriousness on which Brassel seemed continually to balance. For a moment he was buffaloed, his equilibrium disturbed. DeKok never hesitated long, however.

"Dick," he commanded, "call the Greenland Arms."

The three men stood grouped around the phone. Vledder dialed the number. The only sound in the room was the beeping of the touch-tone phone. DeKok's face was serious. Around Brassel's lips played a faint smile, a glow of triumph lit up his light gray eyes.

DeKok listened on an extension.

"Greenland Arms," said a voice, "concierge speaking."

"Police," answered Vledder. "Vledder, Warmoes Street Station. Can you tell me the name of the guest in room twenty-one?"

"One moment, please. Yes, that's Mr. Brets."

"Is he still alive?"

"What did you say?"

"Is Brets still alive?"

A soft chuckle came over the line.

"I handed him his key at eight o'clock."

"That was at eight o'clock. But is he alive *now*?"

"I believe so."

Vledder sighed.

"If it's not too much to ask, would you please take a look in his room?"

"All right. Police, you said? As you wish. Please hold the line."

Meanwhile, DeKok looked at the clock in the detective room. It was a quarter to nine.

It took exactly four minutes until the concierge of the Greenland Arms manifested himself again on the other side of the line.

"Police, police!"

His voice was shaky, anguished.

"Yes?"

"Please send someone here. Mr. Brets...Brets is dead!"

3

Pierre Brassel stepped toward the door.

"I presume," he said with a dismissive gesture, "you gentlemen will have no time for me at the moment. Regrettable. Perhaps another time will be more convenient." He took hold of the doorknob. "In any case, gentlemen, I wish you every possible success with your investigations."

Vledder suddenly seemed to wake up from a daze. Impulsively he leaped at Brassel, grabbing his arm.

"You're not leaving," he said shaking his head. "No, you're not free to walk away, just like that. No, sir! First you'll have to answer a few questions about this killing. Apparently you know a bit too much about it."

The tall, distinguished Brassel, so abruptly prevented from leaving, raised a cautioning finger.

"You do not have the right to manhandle me." There was a barely concealed threat in his tone of voice. "Nor do you have the right to keep me here. The concierge and, perhaps, additional staff of the Greenland Arms will tell you Jan Brets entered the hotel healthy, with his cranium intact. Furthermore, you will hear from the clerk who handed Brets his key shortly thereafter. He will tell you he saw Jan Brets cheerfully depart for his room."

He smiled broadly, a false grin.

"Oh, and I beg to remind you, gentlemen, I have been with the two of you, under your close surveillance, since exactly eight o'clock." He grinned again, mocking and challenging them. He had a twinkle of pure venomous pleasure in his eyes. "What more could you ask? Nobody could wish for a better alibi for a murder case."

Vledder let go of Brassel's arm, but placed himself in front of the door. He stood there like an implacable Cerberus. His boyish face showed a grim, uncompromising expression. It did not seem Pierre Brassel was going to leave without a struggle.

"How did you know," he barked, "that Jan Brets would die in the Greenland Arms tonight? Who, exactly, told you?"

Mr. Brassel gave a bored sigh in response.

"You are wasting your time," he said slowly. "I have already proven abundantly I am *not* the murderer. What more can I tell you?" He grinned maliciously. "Or perhaps you would like me to tell you who killed Jan Brets?"

Vledder nodded, lips pressed together.

"Yes," he hissed from between his teeth, "exactly. That's what I want to know."

Brassel slowly shook his head. His handsome face showed utter contempt.

"But gentlemen," he exclaimed derisively, "where is your professional pride? I should be very disappointed if you did not *insist* on finding Jan Brets's murderer yourselves." His voice was sarcastic, the expression on his face ugly. "Surely the famous Inspector DeKok knows exactly how to proceed. Elementary, you agree? Find the mistakes that have been made."

He paused and looked demonstratively at his watch.

"I am terribly sorry. My time is limited. I have to leave."

He uttered a few more apologies and finally turned toward Vledder.

"If you would be so kind as to step aside so I can pass."

Vledder's face became red. He maintained his stance in front of the door and seemed disinclined to move. Sighing, DeKok rose from his chair. He came from behind his desk and walked over to Vledder.

"Come on, Dick," he commanded gently, "let the gentleman pass. You heard him. The gentleman's time is limited, he has to leave. We should not force our hospitality upon him." He smiled pleasantly, then added, "We won't detain him, not yet. Perhaps another time."

Grudgingly, Vledder stepped aside, a look of hatred in his eyes.

With a courtly bow, Brassel left the room. With an equally courtly bow, DeKok held the door for him.

.

Jan Brets was supine, arms and legs stretched out wide. It was as if he had wanted to cover as much of the floor space as possible. That's how they found him. The position of the corpse made the man resemble a wooden harlequin, a marionette whose every string had been pulled tight. The illusion of a life-sized harlequin struck DeKok. It would not have surprised him in the least if the arms and legs had suddenly started to move rhythmically, guided by the hands of an unseen puppeteer. Adding to the pervasive imagery of a clown was Jan Brets's face. It was waxen and as pale as white greasepaint. It had frozen in an astonished grimace. It seemed Jan Brets, even in death, tried to grasp the joke of his own sudden demise. If it was a joke, he'd just missed the punch line.

The scene may not have struck anyone's funny bone, but it wasn't macabre or fearsome. Death presented itself mildly, without horror. A cursory examination did not even show any overt signs of violence. A small trickle of blood from the left ear ended in a coagulated puddle on the floor. That was all.

"That's exactly how I found him," repeated the concierge in a voice still a bit shrill with excitement. "That was after your, if I may say so, unusual phone call."

DeKok nodded.

"You may say so," he answered amiably. "Please tell me you didn't touch anything."

The concierge shook his head vehemently.

"No, no, Inspector. I didn't touch a thing. Nothing. Well, of course, except the door. But that was hard to avoid. I had to do that. But I didn't go any farther than the door. First I knocked several times. Only after I didn't get an answer did I open the door."

"And?"

"That's when I found him."

"Dead?"

The concierge looked at DeKok with wide-open, scared eyes. He pointed at the floor, his hand shaking.

"Exactly as he is now." His large Adam's apple bobbed up and down and his fingers worried nervously with the buttons of his jacket. "He, eh, he is really dead, isn't he?"

DeKok pursed his lips and nodded.

"He's dead now."

The concierge swallowed quickly.

"You mean he was still alive earlier?"

"You didn't touch the corpse, I mean, you didn't check to see whether he was indeed dead? Did you feel his pulse or check his breathing?"

"No."

DeKok smiled at the subdued face of the concierge. He placed a comforting hand on the man's shoulder.

"He couldn't have been saved anyway," he said soothingly. "Please don't let it bother you, there was nothing you could have done." He gave the man an encouraging smile. "One more thing. Was the room locked when you got here?"

"No." The concierge thought about it. "No, the door wasn't locked. I could just push it open."

"You have a passkey?"

"Yes."

"Who else has one?"

"Almost everybody, except for dining room and kitchen personnel. Maid service, room service, front desk personnel, and myself. Of course, there is also an emergency key for management. Personnel may not use their passkeys except in emergencies. There are very strict rules. We always knock first, for instance. You know what I mean? Nobody wants to barge in on a guest unannounced."

DeKok nodded.

"How many passkeys are available?"

"About twenty."

"And you know exactly who is entitled to have and use such keys?"

"But of course."

"Excellent," murmured DeKok, "very good." Then he continued, a bit louder. "In about half an hour I would like to talk to everyone who has such a key. Get them all together in the reading room." He pushed his hat a bit farther back on his head. "For the time being, you may leave us to do our work. Oh yes, I would also like a list of all the guests, their room numbers, and a floor plan for this floor."

The concierge bowed.

"But of course," he said with professional servility. "Of course, I'll take care of it. I'll take care of it at once." Then he asked, "May I be of service in any other way, gentlemen?"

DeKok grinned at the man and his obvious worry about the hotel's image. The concierge was struck by the way it transformed the inspector's face. A grinning DeKok was irresistible.

"In a moment," said DeKok, smiling, "two rather formidable gentlemen will arrive, dressed in dark coats and accompanied by large leather suitcases."

"Yes?"

"Please welcome them in my name and have them immediately conveyed to this room. Those two gentlemen, you see, are the world's greatest experts in photographing corpses and taking fingerprints."

"Oh," said the concierge.

"Yes," agreed DeKok. "And in case," he continued, "you spot any gentlemen of the press, you will be so kind as to deny them access past the porter's lodge. Understood?"

The concierge bowed obsequiously.

"Excellent," said DeKok, "thank you very much." He closed the door of room twenty-one in the face of the bewildered concierge.

Vledder had been roaming the scene of the crime for some time as DeKok finished his conversation with the concierge. He had inspected the bolts on the French doors to the balcony and was now busily engaged in a number of measurements to determine the exact position of the corpse. He compiled it all into a sketch of the crime scene.

When DeKok turned away from the door, Vledder pointed at a hockey stick on the floor next to it. This was an unusual kind of hockey stick. Apart from the usual tape on the handle, the blade, too, was heavily wrapped. The tape around the blade was newer, obviously applied rather recently.

DeKok took a clean handkerchief from a pocket and lifted the stick between thumb and index finger. It almost slipped from his fingers. The stick was unusually heavy.

"What on earth?" he exclaimed, surprise in his voice. "This stick has been weighted. Something heavy, perhaps lead, has been attached to the blade. It's hard to see at the moment, but I bet next year's salary the bottom tape has no other purpose than to keep weights in place."

He looked at it closely.

"You know, young Vledder," he remarked after a while, "I think this particular murder took some time in the planning. It's the result of a well-conceived, detailed scheme. Look at the hockey stick, for instance. The new tape has been very carefully applied. At first glance I'd say that it's the result of several hours' work."

He sighed sadly.

"I'd say it has been altered with care and devotion better applied to more productive labor. The killer, whoever he or she may be, obviously took pride in the preparatory work."

Vledder did not react to the musings of his mentor. He did not seem interested. He sulked. There was an obstreperous look on his face. It did not escape DeKok. He replaced the stick where he had found it and walked over to Vledder.

"What's the matter, Dick?" he asked pleasantly. "Aren't you satisfied with the course of events?"

Vledder stood up, his measuring tape in hand.

"No," he said, annoyed. "I'm not satisfied with the course of events—not at all. I think you made a serious mistake."

DeKok made a helpless gesture.

"I'm really not aware of having made a mistake." It sounded like an apology. "Tell me, what mistake was that?"

"You shouldn't have let Pierre Brassel just get away!"

The old inspector sighed deeply.

"So *that's* what's eating you," he said. His tone was resigned. "I thought so back at the office." He rubbed his broad face, then raised a cautioning finger. "Just take it from me, Dick, a policeman should always be extremely careful with intelligent people. They can cause a lot more trouble than the not so bright ones. Pierre Brassel is extremely intelligent, much more intelligent than you think. He's fully aware of what he's doing. Even if we don't yet understand his motives, his background, that's *our* fault. That's a lack of insight on our part for which we have nobody to blame but ourselves, certainly not our friend Brassel."

"That's not the issue," exclaimed Vledder sharply. "That's not the point! We should just have kept him and we should have interrogated him until he told us exactly what we wanted to know."

Eyebrows rippling like woolly caterpillars, DeKok looked thoughtfully at his partner. "You don't believe," said DeKok finally, "that we can force someone to tell us things he doesn't want to tell us. It's an ethical question with limits that every policeman must determine for himself." He paused. "For the sake of argument, however, please state the legal grounds on which we could have kept Brassel in custody."

"He knew about the murder."

DeKok nodded calmly.

"Certainly, on that we agree. What else?"

Vledder looked at him with amazement.

"What else? Even had we been unable to charge him as an accomplice, he still had the legal obligation to warn the police a crime was about to be committed. Let's see, how exactly is that phrased? Oh yes, 'at a time sufficient to prevent the commission of the crime.' He didn't do that.

While he was acting the charlatan in the detective room, mouthing all sorts of nonsense, he calmly allowed the victim to be murdered in this room."

Vledder became more and more agitated. The blood rushed to his head. Nervous tics developed on his cheeks.

"Damn it!" he cried, knowing full well DeKok disapproved of strong language. "He knew where and how it was going to happen. Jan Brets was going to have his skull cracked in room twenty-one, the Greenland Arms. He knew it as well as if he had done it himself."

"And is that possible?" asked DeKok seriously. "Could Pierre Brassel have killed Jan Brets?"

Vledder sighed.

"No," he admitted reluctantly. "Not if the concierge spoke the truth about seeing Jan Brets alive at precisely eight o'clock."

DeKok nodded.

"Exactly," he said. "If we take that as our starting point, possibly we'll find additional witnesses who can corroborate. If Jan Brets was still alive at eight o'clock, then no matter how much you regret it, Pierre Brassel could not possibly have committed the murder."

DeKok looked around the room. Then he continued, "I haven't seen any ingenious remote-control apparatus. The hockey stick was handled in an orthodox manner. I mean, someone lifted the stick high with both hands and brought it down hard enough to break Brets's head. That someone could not possibly have been Brassel."

He placed a fatherly hand on Vledder's shoulder.

"Apart from that, you're absolutely right. Brassel knew the murder was about to be committed. He did indeed have the legal obligation to inform someone, whether police or victim…"

Vledder shot DeKok a questioning look.

"What do you mean?"

"Exactly what I'm saying: he must warn one or the other, police or victim. The law provides for either opportunity. Pierre Brassel is *not* guilty if he warned the victim in time. Obviously it would have to be timely."

Vledder made a wild, uncontrolled gesture.

"But, DeKok," he cried, irritated, "surely you know he didn't warn the victim either. Otherwise this wouldn't have happened."

DeKok raised a restraining hand.

"Wait a moment. We have no proof. It's entirely possible the murderer warned Jan Brets. Maybe Brets chose to ignore the warning, considering it to be a bad joke. Remember how you reacted to Brassel's letter? You thought it was a sick joke." He shook his head. "No, Vledder," he sighed, "we can't do a thing about Brassel under the present circumstances. Any action would result in incarceration, and that is a terrible word."

4

DeKok pointed at the corpse on the floor.

"Well, Bram, what do you think of our harlequin?"

Bram Weelen, the rotund police photographer, forced his lips into a grin.

"Yes, well, a harlequin," he grinned again. "You're right, that's what it looks like, a doll with strings. In my opinion, his assailant posed him in this manner. Let's face it, it's hardly a natural position."

DeKok chewed his lower lip.

"You ever see this before?"

Bram shook his head.

"Never. I have not seen anything like it before. I've photographed a lot of corpses, but this is singular, and not a little strange."

He walked carefully around the corpse.

"What was the cause of death?"

DeKok pointed at the hockey stick.

"It's almost certain this was the murder weapon, a hockey stick, probably weighted with lead. It was used to bash his head in. Look at the blood from the left ear. It almost certainly indicates an injury to the base of the cranium. I haven't looked any closer. We're waiting for

Dr. Rusteloos. I expect he's on the way. Perhaps he can give us some clarification about the strange position. It really intrigues me."

Bram nodded.

"Yes, it's pretty weird. As I said, I've never seen a body posed this way." He called to Kruger, the fingerprint expert. "Hey, Ben, you ever seen anything like this?"

Kruger shook his head. His face, always melancholic, was particularly solemn.

"No," he said sadly. "It's a new one to me, too."

Bram grimaced toward DeKok.

"And I've had to work with that for the last umpteen years." It sounded like a lament. With a sigh he unpacked his Hasselblad. He started taking the usual shots, wide-angles, snapshots, detailed close-ups. Bram used his camera with the eyes and hands of a master. He was an artist who had accidentally strayed into police work.

Meticulous in his own way, Kruger quickly finished with his dusting and search for prints. The hotel room was not very big. After his virtuoso performance with the brush, the catch was minute.

It took about twenty minutes for both experts to finish. Each completed his rather grim ritual by donning his dark overcoat. Then each hefted his heavy suitcase and disappeared in silence and efficiency. Kruger did not even bother to say good-bye. Bram turned at the door.

"If I were you, DeKok," he said, pointing at the corpse, "I'd look for a sinister joker."

"Where do you suggest?"

Bram pushed his lower lip forward.

"That's your business."
DeKok waved him away.
"Thanks for the tip."

Although DeKok was used to working with Dr. Koning, Dr. Rusteloos was a respected man in his field. DeKok appreciated his direct nature and was not offended when Rusteloos wasted little time on greetings. He immediately lowered himself on one knee and started to explore the body with his sensitive fingers. When he turned the head of the victim slightly, the damage to the skull was clearly visible.

"This was quite a blow," he said, studying the edges of the wound. "As far as I can see, it was but a single blow." He smiled bitterly. "But one blow was more than enough."

DeKok showed him the hockey stick.

"Could this have been the weapon, doctor? The stick has been weighted at the bottom."

Dr. Rusteloos looked intently at the weapon.

"I believe so," he said carefully, "but I can't give you a definite opinion at this time, you understand. I want to do a more careful examination of the body, but at first glance the stick could very well have been used as the weapon. Superficially, I'd say the wound could have been caused by such a device."

DeKok nodded thoughtfully.

"And doctor," he continued, "what about the position of the victim? The position of the arms and legs? Is that normal? I mean, if somebody collapsed after a fatal blow on the head, would it be reasonable to expect the body to assume that position?"

Slowly Dr. Rusteloos shook his head.

"No," he said hesitantly, "it's most unusual. I've never seen anything like it." He stared pensively at the corpse. "Strange indeed, a strange pose. It reminds me of something. It reminds me of—"

"A marionette, a harlequin," completed DeKok.

"Exactly right, yes, a harlequin."

It sounded comical coming from him.

Further investigations in the hotel did not produce much. The personnel had very little to say. The management had accounted for all the passkeys; not one key was missing, and everyone had the keys he or she was supposed to have. An elderly elevator operator corroborated the concierge's statement: Mr. Brets had entered the hotel at eight o'clock or, at most, five minutes later. He had picked up his key at the desk, and the elderly operator had conveyed him to the third floor. He had even observed Brets walking down the corridor to his room. The doors had closed, and the elevator had again descended. Nobody had entered the lift on Brets's floor. In any case, with the exception of Mr. Brets, the witness had seen nobody else on the third floor.

By looking at the register, they learned Brets had arrived three days earlier. He was registered as Jan Johannes Brets, age twenty-five, merchant, 315 Brooklyn Street, Utrecht. The front desk clerk had assumed the name was correct because the guest had used a passport for identification. The register contained the passport number. It would have been simple to check the accuracy of the number with a single phone call.

Brets had checked in with almost no luggage. There was a small carry-on bag found under the bed, nothing remarkable. However, the contents of the bag *were* remarkable. It contained an extensive, well-maintained selection of burglary tools.

In the process of interrogation, the investigators learned Brets had not mingled with the other guests. He hadn't associated with anybody. As far as anyone knew, he received no visitors in his room. His only meals at the hotel had been breakfasts. For the rest of each day he had been absent. His behavior had not prompted management to pay particular attention; his comings and goings had been like those of any guest on business.

DeKok found it all very disheartening. The investigation in the Greenland Arms could be considered a dud. Once more, DeKok addressed the concierge.

"Did anybody ask for Mr. Brets around eight o'clock?"

"At the desk, or with the doorman?"

"Either."

The concierge was obviously trying to remember.

"No, not as far as I know."

"Telephone?"

The concierge's face cleared up.

"Yes, just a moment, somebody called."

"What time?"

"It must have been shortly after eight."

"Who called?"

The concierge shrugged his shoulders.

"That I don't know. The caller did not mention a name. It was a woman. She asked if Mr. Brets was in."

"And?"

"Well, I answered yes, because I had just seen him pick up the key. I asked if I should call him or ring his room, but she answered, 'Never mind' and broke the connection."

DeKok nodded slowly.

"You have some experience with this sort of phone call. Tell me, was it his mother, his wife, a fiancée, a lover?"

The concierge smiled.

"That's difficult to say," he sighed. "It didn't seem to be any of those. If I had to guess, I'd say there was no intimate relationship. The lady sounded cooler, business-like. She sounded a bit hurried...maybe nervous." He paused and was lost in thought. "There was something about the voice," he added after a while. "There was something about the voice," he repeated.

"What?"

The concierge pulled on his lower lip, mulling over his recollection. Suddenly he looked up. "I've got it," he said happily. "I remember now. The voice had a German accent. You know what I mean, a German who's been living in Holland for years, speaks perfect Dutch but yet you can hear..."

DeKok nodded.

"I understand."

The attendants from the coroner's office entered. They pushed the arms and legs of the harlequin into a straight line, slid the body into a body bag, and placed it on the stretcher. DeKok watched their movements intently.

After the corpse had been removed, DeKok made a last round of the room. Then he locked the door and sealed it.

In the meantime, Vledder checked to see how much time it would take to go from the entrance of the hotel to room twenty-one. It took exactly four minutes, including knocking on the door.

After more than three hours, the inspectors finally left the Greenland Arms.

It was quiet in the streets. Vledder and DeKok headed for the station house on foot. Vledder carried the hockey stick and the athletic bag of burglary tools. They crossed Damrak, one of the wider streets in Amsterdam. It was nearly deserted. Damrak led to the dam, a large square that was popular as a hippie gathering place during the sixties.

DeKok followed his young partner. Because of his duck-footed waddle, he was behind by a few paces. His old, decrepit felt hat was pushed to the back of his head as he walked and thought. Meanwhile, he whistled a Christmas carol with sharply pursed lips. "Oh, come all ye faithful." He was distinctly off key. He always whistled off key, and always Christmas carols, regardless of the time of year. In the center of the large square he suddenly halted. Involuntary thoughts drifted toward Christmas presents. He recalled the previous Christmas. Then he walked on.

"No harlequin under the tree," he murmured.

5

DeKok nursed his tired feet. He leaned comfortably back in his chair, both feet on his desk, and sucked a peppermint. He thought about the days when under such circumstances he would have taken a perverse delight in tipping the ash from his cigar onto the freshly waxed floor of the detective room. Alas, his smoking days were over. These days he only smoked for a purpose, sometimes to annoy a suspect or to form a bond between himself and an overwrought witness. As much as he disliked role-playing, it went with the territory.

The sudden demise of the merchant from Utrecht did not cause him any particular sorrow. He was not exactly upset about it. No matter how he searched his conscience, he was unable to discover a trace of pity, sorrow, or grief. Nonetheless, Jan Brets was a murder victim. Now DeKok was professionally involved. In a civilized society it is simply not permitted to break the skull of one's fellow man.

He could not, however, fail to be intrigued by the how and why of the deed. Murderers do not, with rare exception, kill on sheer impulse. There had to be a purpose, a goal, a motive. What could it be?

DeKok pulled a wrinkled, official-looking envelope from his inside pocket. He took out an equally wrinkled note. He handed it carefully to Vledder, who sat across from him and slowly sipped a cup of coffee.

"What is it?"

DeKok grinned.

"Found under the corpse of Brets. I saw it while the attendants moved the corpse."

Vledder looked at the note with mounting amazement.

"Isn't…isn't that Brassel's writing?"

DeKok nodded.

"Apparently. It's a vaguely worded warning to the victim. It may just be enough to keep him legally immune. Just read it."

Vledder read out loud: "'My dear Mr. Brets, I advise you not to enter your hotel room after eight o'clock on Wednesday night. Stay away. Otherwise a deadly surprise will await you.' He signed it 'Pierre Brassel.'" Vledder returned the note to DeKok.

"And you found it under the corpse?"

"Yes."

"Not in one of his pockets?"

"No."

"Don't you find it rather strange? If someone delivered the note to Brets in the usual way, I mean, if somebody handed it to him, he would have put it in a pocket, don't you think?"

DeKok nodded thoughtfully.

"Indeed, it would be the most obvious thing to do. Therefore I suspect Jan Brets never saw this so-called warning himself. Presumably the murderer placed the note at the scene, just as he posed the body—*after* the murder. He wanted us to find the note during our crime scene investigation."

Vledder added, "If it was Brassel, he was trying to ensure we could not charge him for concealing knowledge of a murder. As you explained earlier, he wanted us to believe he fulfilled a legal obligation to warn the victim."

DeKok nodded approvingly at Vledder.

"And that's the way it is, Dick. This murderer planned absolutely everything. It's perfect in a macabre way. I'm tempted to say almost flawless."

Vledder looked surprised.

"Almost?"

DeKok rubbed his hands through his bristly hair.

"Murderers always make mistakes," he sighed. "Always. There has *got* to be a mistake somewhere."

He made a lazy gesture.

"If I were suddenly to believe in the perfect crime, I would immediately resign from the force."

Vledder sat down at his desk and called central registry in Utrecht. The stream of information seemed unstoppable. He had difficulty making all the necessary notes. When he finally replaced the receiver, he sighed with relief.

"And what," asked DeKok, interested, "did our friends in Utrecht tell you about Jan Brets?"

Vledder grimaced.

"Well," he said with a broad grin on his face, "nobody in Utrecht seems to be grieving his death. Tomorrow it seems the commissaris intends to treat the entire force to champagne."

DeKok laughed heartily.

"All that bad?"

Vledder consulted his notes and made some entries on his computer keyboard. Soon a number of sheets came out of the printer. He studied the sheets for a moment and then made a few more entries on his computer. With one of the sheets in hand, he turned to his partner.

"Yes, that bad," he answered seriously. "Over the years Mr. Brets has given the Utrecht police a run for their money. Here is a sample of his rap sheet. In his relatively short life, he managed to break almost all of the Lord's commandments—theft, breaking and entering, robbery, everything, even murder."

DeKok grinned.

"Nice guy."

Vledder nodded.

"A prince of a guy. As far as I can see, he's spent more time in jail than out."

DeKok looked thoughtfully at nothing in particular.

"Did I understand correctly," he said, "did you say there was a murder on his sheet?"

"Yes."

"Does it give details?"

Vledder studied his notes again.

"Let's see. Yes, here it is. He was seventeen and incarcerated. The youth reform institution in Haarlem gave him a weekend pass for good behavior. Brets and an eighteen-year-old accomplice from the institution broke into a house. The victim, an elderly man, resisted the illegal intrusion. They murdered him. The take from the robbery, according to the report, was less than ten euros."

DeKok shook his head sadly.

"Shocking," he sighed, "just terrible. Less than ten euros for a man's life." He sighed again. "He was not on parole or anything?"

Vledder nodded.

"Oh, yes, he hadn't escaped. When Jan Brets was killed, he was free as a bird."

DeKok moved into a more comfortable position.

"Why," he asked, slightly puzzled, "wasn't he punished for the murder?"

Vledder shrugged his shoulders.

"I readily assume he was punished," he answered bitterly. "In a manner that has lately become the norm in our friendly little country: with the utmost of humanity and understanding. He was underage, you know. He was arrested several times after the murder but has gone to trial only twice. Both trials related to a series of burglaries."

Lost in a sea of thought, DeKok stared out of the window for a long time.

"Ach," he said finally, his voice grave. "What do you expect? Crime, punishment, vengeance, they're all old-fashioned concepts. We live in a new era. It's more fashionable to feel pity for the criminal; it seems we've become more and more forgiving."

"You mean we've spawned more and more criminals," Vledder said grimly. "Crime is getting people in the spotlight. It's almost a respectable hobby."

The young inspector snorted.

"*Sir,*" he spoke suddenly in a strange, high-pitched voice, "*what do you do in your spare time?* Who, me? Well, I'm sort of a criminal. You know, every Saturday night I do a little breaking and entering, maybe hold up a gas station, just to calm down. Then, perhaps once a month, a murder helps me relax completely, get rid of the stress. *Well, don't the police do anything about that?* Of course they almost always try to stop me. You see, I have a number of phobias and other complexes. The psychiatrists and judges usually set me free immediately. I seldom even need bail. You see, my criminal escapades help me socially."

DeKok laughed.

"Come, come, Dick," he said in a friendly, soothing manner, "don't be so cynical. It isn't quite that bad. You exaggerate. Anyway, the sentencing and punishing of criminals has nothing to do with us. As policemen, it's none of our business—happily so. Let's concentrate on Jan Brets and his untimely demise."

Vledder nodded sober agreement.

"You're right," Vledder assented reluctantly. "It truly is a waste of time to get upset about the judicial system. Also, I admit to being a bit prejudiced."

DeKok smiled.

"I once knew an old detective who would go crazy every time he had a case. His greatest desire was to put *everybody* behind bars so that the police could live quietly."

Amazed, Vledder looked at his mentor.

"Did he mean that?"

DeKok grinned.

"I think so, but it occurred to me that he was also very, very lazy."

The phone rang at that moment and Vledder lifted the receiver.

"For you," he said after listening to the voice at the other end of the line. "It's the concierge from the Greenland Arms."

DeKok relieved him of the receiver.

"Yes?"

"There are two long-distance calls in the records for Mr. Brets," said the concierge. "Both calls were to Utrecht, to number 271228. We discovered the charges while we were in the process of closing out Mr. Brets's account. The entire bill is a loss, or do you think the family..."

DeKok ignored the remark. He was a master at ignoring things when he felt like it.

"Utrecht," he repeated, "two-seven-one-double two-eight."

"Does it help you?"

"That's difficult to say. In any case, many thanks."

He broke the connection.

"You heard the number, Dick?"

Vledder nodded.

DeKok began to pace up and down the large detective room. Something was bothering him. He halted at his favorite spot, in front of the window. He looked toward Corner Alley. His eyebrows danced dangerously, a deep frown wrinkled his forehead. He pondered a number of strange facets of Jan Brets's murder. There weren't many things he'd never encountered, at one time or another, in his long career. Again, he let the known facts pass through in his mind.

"Jan Brets," he murmured to himself, "a character with, let's say, a certain notoriety, checks into a hotel. Upon returning to the hotel one day, someone brutally attacks and murders Brets in his hotel room. The killer probably waited behind the door, approached him from the rear, and bashed in his skull. There was no evidence of a struggle. Brets was completely surprised. The murder weapon, a hockey stick, had been prepared sometime in advance. Therefore the murderer carefully planned his crime. We have the strange note from Brassel confirming his plan to murder Brets. The motive, the only thing that could possibly shed any light on it all, is a complete mystery."

He paused to sigh, then resumed his soliloquy.

"We do not know a great deal about the victim, except he specialized in burglaries during the last few years. We found the tools of his trade in the hotel room. We could presume the victim was in Amsterdam to commit a burglary."

Again he paused, rubbed his hands through his hair.

"But then," he said louder and more slowly, "the question remains whether he was alone."

Vledder shrugged his shoulders.

"Possibly," he answered. "Or perhaps Brets was only here to reconnoiter the terrain and wait to meet his accomplices. Maybe he was just on a fact-finding tour, so to speak."

DeKok nodded.

"Yes," he said thoughtfully, "that's possible. Jan Brets's sheet indicates he wasn't the type to do jobs on his own.

He always had accomplices. Thus there must be others who are aware of the plan."

"A plan for a break-in somewhere?"

"Exactly, Dick, the plan for a break-in, as you put it, a burglary, a robbery, somewhere in Amsterdam. It must have been something big, requiring careful planning. Let's face it. Brets didn't leave his normal haunts in Utrecht to come to Amsterdam for something minor. It is interesting, too, when a man like Brets takes a room in the Greenland Arms. It is certainly several levels above his normal choice of lodgings. It must mean something."

Vledder stared at nothing in particular. "You're right," he said slowly. "It had to be something special. And I wouldn't be at all surprised if his sudden death had something to do with it."

DeKok gestured.

"It seems a bit premature to come to such a conclusion. We really should wait until we know a little more. For instance, if Brets came here intending to commit a crime, was there a plan? If so, what did he or they plan to do? Who were the participants? More important, what induced Brets to come to Amsterdam? Did he get a tip? If so, who was the tipster? Remember, Brets is an unknown in the Amsterdam underworld. This is the first I've heard of him."

Vledder shook his head.

"Same here, although that doesn't mean much. But what worries me is how Brassel fits into all of this."

DeKok sighed.

"Perhaps he's the brain behind it all, the designer of the plan. Who knows?"

Vledder looked searchingly at his older colleague.

"Then how do you explain the murder?"

DeKok did not answer. He stared outside. His face was expressionless. Suddenly he turned around and walked to the peg on the wall.

"Come on, Dick," he said, surrounding himself with his old raincoat. "I think we should make a trip to Utrecht."

Vledder's face betrayed his astonishment.

DeKok showed a serious face.

"It's never too late to console an old mother on the loss of her son."

6

Vledder and DeKok stood on the sidewalk belonging to a long line of row houses on a dismal street in Utrecht. They approached one of the houses and rang the bell several times. They banged on the door for good measure. Finally, an unkempt female appeared at one of the windows. DeKok looked up in the gloom.

"Mrs. Brets?"

"Yes." She sounded cross, not to say belligerent.

"I'm sorry, ma'am," said DeKok in a friendly tone of voice. "I'm really sorry to wake you. But we need to talk to you."

"Now, in the middle of the night?"

"Yes, it's very important."

"I'm not home for nobody," she yelled from above. "Nobody, you hear? If you don't go away, I'll call the police."

DeKok coughed.

"We, eh, we *are* the police."

"Oh?"

"Yes."

"What do you want?"

"It's about your son."

"About Jan?"

DeKok started to get a crick in his neck from staring up at the window.

"Yes," he yelled back, "about Jan!"

"What's the matter with him?"

DeKok sighed deeply. This shouting match on a quiet street was not to his liking. Before long the whole neighborhood would be awake.

"Would you mind letting us in?" he asked compellingly. "This is a bit difficult, like this."

"All right then, hold on a minute."

The head disappeared.

A few minutes later they could hear stumbling on the ground floor. A light appeared in the corridor, and after a lot of rattling of chains and bolts, the door finally opened.

"Come in and don't look at the mess. I haven't had a chance to clean downstairs."

She shuffled away.

DeKok murmured something along the lines of "Who cares?" and waddled after the woman into the house. Vledder followed.

The woman was skinny and rawboned. Gray, thin hair framed her face in stringy strands. She'd hastily thrown a raincoat over her nightgown, a pale pink ruffle peeked out of the placket. Thin white legs emerged from beneath the raincoat and ended in old formless slippers. The slippers were several sizes too large, causing her to slide rather than walk. She led them to a small parlor where she sank down, shivering, on a stained sofa in front of a cold fireplace.

"Sit down," she invited with a grand gesture. "Put the dirty laundry on the floor somewhere. I should have washed today, but I didn't get to it. I haven't felt at all well the last few days. I may have something wrong with my back; arthritis, I think." She sighed deeply. "Ach," she added sadly, "when you get older, these things happen. The years take their toll, you can't stop it. Old churches have dim windows."

DeKok nodded agreement. He pushed the pile of laundry aside and sat down next to her.

"My name is DeKok," he said amicably. "DeKok with, eh, a kay-oh-kay. This is my colleague Vledder. We're police inspectors from Amsterdam."

"Oh," she said, "from Amsterdam?"

She seemed used to police visits. It was a matter of supreme indifference to her. Only the fact that they came from Amsterdam seemed to arouse a vague curiosity.

"Amsterdam," she repeated, "Amsterdam."

DeKok nodded. Meanwhile, he bit his lower lip nervously. He was still looking for words, had not formulated his thoughts properly. The old woman looked at him. In order to escape her questioning glance, he looked around at Vledder, who leaned against the mantelpiece. The woman felt his hesitation.

"Well, what's up with Jan? Arrested?"

She cackled.

DeKok rubbed the back of his hand over his mouth. It was difficult to define the situation with Brets. He thought about it.

"No," he answered slowly, "he's not been arrested."

"What then?"

She scooted a little closer.

"It, eh, it's something else. We found Jan in a hotel earlier tonight. He...he's not well. Not well at all."

She looked at him with sharp eyes.

"What's the matter with him?"

DeKok swallowed.

"What's the matter with Jan?" she asked again in her belligerent voice. "You can tell me, you know. I don't get shocked that easily. Not anymore. I've learned to roll with the punches. With Jan it's one thing or another, and most of it isn't good."

DeKok swallowed again.

"Jan, eh, Jan is dead."

She did not change visibly. Her long, sinewy fingers reached for a pack of cigarettes and some matches on the round table in front of her.

"So," she said resignedly, "so it finally happened." She lit a cigarette with shaking hands. She inhaled deeply. "It finally happened," she repeated. Her voice sounded strange, as if from a distance.

Slowly she let the smoke escape.

"I should have expected it," she murmured. "You know, it was to be expected. I'm not all that surprised, no, not surprised." She shook her head. "It had to happen, sooner or later." She sounded melancholy, almost wistful.

Vledder and DeKok listened to the rambling mono-logue. They allowed her to deal with the news in her own way. Silently they watched as she crushed the cigarette in the ashtray after a few puffs. She moved slowly, with exaggerated caution. She kept crushing the cigarette, long after it had been extinguished.

Slowly her attitude changed. The iron grip of her self-control relented slightly. At first the shock seemed to come from deep within her. The sobs were unstoppable, like hiccups. Suddenly she clasped both hands in front of her eyes and started to cry. Her whole body shook violently.

DeKok felt a deep pity. He placed an arm around her bony shoulders and pulled her softly toward him. She did not resist. She cried her sorrow with long wails from an asthmatic chest. She was a poor, pitiful, much plagued woman, a mother of a failed son.

It took a long time before she calmed down. She picked up a dirty shirt from the floor and used it to wipe her tears.

"How," she asked finally, "did it happen? Or is that a secret?"

DeKok sighed.

"Of course it's not a secret."

"Well?" she urged.

DeKok did not answer at once. He looked at her from the side and tried to estimate her resistance, her ability to absorb another shock.

"Jan was murdered."

"Murdered?"

"Yes."

She gave him a bitter smile.

"To tell you the truth, I was thinking the police might have killed him."

DeKok's eyebrows rippled.

"Why the police?"

She shook her thin shoulders.

"It was the most obvious. It could have happened."

DeKok grinned, a bit embarrassed.

"I don't understand," he said.

"Ach," she said, suddenly irritated, "forget it! What does it matter now? He's dead. Why bother, what's past is past."

DeKok sighed. He seemed to do a lot of that, he reflected.

"Listen," he said seriously, "it's not a pleasant thing to do, but it's probably better if you know the facts. You'll hear them sooner or later anyway. Somebody, we don't know who, beat Jan on the head with a heavy object. It was murder. My colleague and I are in charge of the investigation. It's not going to be easy to find Jan's killer. We don't have many clues. We hoped you could help us."

The expression on her face changed. The mildness, the softness caused by sorrow slowly disappeared. It was as if she suddenly realized who was speaking to her. Policemen. And not for the first time in her life, either. The memories of the past left a bitter taste in her mouth.

"Why?" she asked suspiciously. "Why should I help the police?"

"Because it's your civic duty," answered DeKok carefully.

She grinned. It was not a pleasant sight.

"My *duty*?" She pronounced it like an obscenity.

DeKok swallowed.

"Because it concerns your son," he amplified.

"And it will bring him back?"

DeKok narrowed his eyes.

"No," he said, suddenly sharp. "No, that won't bring your son back. I'm not God. I can't make that sort of deal with you. I'd hoped, however, that your son's death would teach you something. Apparently I was mistaken."

He stood up and walked out of the room.

"Come on," he said to Vledder over his shoulder, "let's go. There's no sense in staying. We're wasting our time."

She hastily rose and shuffled after him. She overtook him in the corridor and grabbed the back of his coat.

"When is he coming home, sir?" It sounded pleading, almost scared. "Mister, when do I get my boy back home? He'll be buried here, won't he?"

Slowly DeKok turned. Her words hurt him. He already regretted how sharp his words had been, losing his temper. He looked down at her, meeting her gaze. He had a lump in his throat he couldn't dislodge. Her face again reflected mild tenderness, only expressed by an old mother. DeKok had no defense against it. He placed his hand on the gray head.

"I'll take care of it myself," he said softly. "Jan will be buried here."

A soft smile played over her face.

"Thank you," she said simply.

They took their leave.

Before the inspectors stepped into the street, she added, "Go see Fat Anton, he may be able to tell you something. He and Jan used to spend a lot of time together." She sighed. "Tell Anton I sent you," she added.

She closed the door and shuffled back to the room.

7

Fat Anton did honor to his name.

He was enormous, with a triple chin. His small, recessed pig's eyes glittered above round cheeks.

He had not taken the trouble to rise. He received the inspectors while in bed. Next to his thigh, hidden by blankets, was a mound in the shape of a woman. Only the top of her head was visible. Fat Anton scratched somewhere under his T-shirt.

"Well," he said, yawning, "Ma Brets sent you and Jan got banged on the head in Amsterdam?"

"Indeed," answered DeKok laconically. "In a nutshell."

Anton looked confused.

"Well, just tell me," he asked, challenging, "what's that got to do with me?"

DeKok shook his head.

"Nothing, absolutely nothing."

Anton's round face became more cheerful. He spread a pair of mighty arms and looked at DeKok with indignation.

"Well, then what do you want?"

Without waiting to be invited, DeKok sat down at the foot of the bed.

"Listen to me, Anton," he began amiably, "we have reason to believe that Jan Brets did not stay at the Greenland Arms for fun. He was there working on a job. The Greenland Arms is a boutique hotel, so we believe it was an important job. In other words, he was there for a rich haul."

Fat Anton grinned.

"I like the way you think," he said admiringly.

DeKok rubbed his face with the flat of his hand and sighed deeply. He understood full well that he was not getting any further this way. He decided to change his tactics.

"Jan Brets," he said patiently, "was your best friend, right?"

Fat Anton nodded emphatically.

"Yes, sir, he was," he agreed.

"Excellent," said DeKok. "That helps. Well, your best friend, Jan Brets, is dead, murdered. Somebody was nasty enough to break his skull."

"A dirty trick," reacted Anton spontaneously. "They shouldn't have done that."

DeKok swallowed.

"Yes, Anton," he said, his voice catching in his throat, "you're right, a dirty trick. That's why I'm asking you, his best friend, whether it's possible his murderer had anything to do with a job."

Anton thought deeply. It was visible. He rubbed a greasy hand over stubbly hair. A painful expression appeared on his face.

"It's possible," he said after a while. "It's possible, but I don't think so."

"Why not?"

"Nobody knew about the job."

DeKok sighed.

"Anton, *you* knew about it." There was amazement in his voice and on his face.

"Well, yes, of course. I was part of it."

"Part of what?"

Fat Anton blinked his eyes several times in rapid succession and then laughed sheepishly. "Well, you got me, eh? You got me. I never can shut my big mouth!"

DeKok ignored the remark.

"Go on," he said, "you were part of what?"

"Part of the gang." It sounded reluctant.

"What gang would that be?"

Fat Anton shrugged his colossal shoulders.

"Well, you know, *gang* sounds impressive...real American, you know. It was just a few of the guys."

"What guys?"

Anton shook his head.

"You got it, Inspector," he said with irritation in his voice. "Jan and I belonged to a *group*, all right? I already said too much, so you shouldn't ask anymore. That's useless. I won't give you the other names anyway."

DeKok smiled a winning smile.

"Oh, well," he said, "we won't discuss it anymore. You don't want to betray anybody, and I understand that." He took a deep breath. "Just one more thing, what sort of haul are we talking about?"

Fat Anton looked reluctant.

"I'd rather not say."

DeKok looked at him evenly.

"What you mean," he said knowingly, "is that with Jan or without him, you and the others will finish the job." He made an expressive gesture. "I understand," he continued. "There will be a larger share for everybody else."

Suddenly a female head emerged from the blankets next to Anton. The young woman had black curly hair. Streaks of makeup ran down her pale face. Obviously she had heard the entire conversation from under the blankets.

"You," she announced decidedly, "you're no longer part of it. Not you. I don't care what the others do, that's their business. But you're out of it. To hell with the whole mess! I never trusted this setup. Now you see it yourself. Jan Brets is already dead. You could have listened to me and Jan when I said not to trust the jerk. He's disgusting—" Fat Anton tried to push her head back under the blankets. "He's such a fine gentleman," she managed to add.

"Shut up, Marie," growled Anton. "Stay out of this. It's none of your business."

"What fine gentleman?" asked DeKok, very much interested.

"Well," said Marie vehemently, "the accountant, the jerk who gave Brets the tip in the first place, of course."

"I beg your pardon?" DeKok tried to believe what he was hearing.

"Yes, the accountant. Come on, Anton, what was his name again?"

"Pierre Brassel?" asked DeKok hopefully.

Marie's pale face brightened up.

"That's him exactly, Pierre Brassel."

DeKok stood in front of the window of the detective room, both hands folded behind his back. The early morning light already stole through Corner Alley. The birds on the roof of Warmoes Street sang and chirped in a tone so clear and pure, it was as if they were in a quiet monastery garden rather than just above one of the seamiest districts in Europe.

"What an evening, what a night," sighed DeKok. "One for the books. Barely ten hours ago, Brassel walked in here and we stepped into this morass."

He rolled back and forth a few times on the balls of his feet in an attempt to drive the leaden feeling out of his calves.

"We got a break when Inspector Meyden in Utrecht was able to tell us at once where we could find Fat Anton. I'm not all that familiar with the Utrecht under-world. It might have taken us a long time to find him on our own."

Vledder came and stood next to him.

"Really," he said sadly, "we've not made any progress with the investigation. Fat Anton was not exactly a gold mine of information."

Smiling, DeKok shook his head.

"That Anton," he said, grinning at the recollection, "what a mountain of flesh. He almost needed the entire king-sized bed by himself. The man's a colossus!"

Vledder nodded.

"Too bad, despite everything, he didn't want to tell us who else is involved. They could still be targeting someone or something unknown."

"Yes," agreed DeKok, "it's too bad. I would have given a week's salary to find out what sort of tip Brassel passed along. It must have been something the boys liked very much. To form any sort of gang, or even a 'group of guys,' is not all that common in this country. The Dutch criminal is by nature a pure individualist. He doesn't form groups; at most he'll work with a single partner."

Vledder made a gesture.

"You know," he said, "when NATO conducts exercises, the story is the Dutch army always gets the lowest ratings in unit maneuvers, but the Dutch soldier is always rated first in guerilla warfare. Perhaps with the inspired leadership of Pierre Brassel, the so-called gang managed to overcome their natural aversion to cooperation. Who knows what he promised them."

DeKok looked at his watch.

"It's almost six o'clock. I propose we first get a few hours' sleep. We've had enough for one day. I asked the Utrecht police to send me the complete file on Jan Brets. They promised to deliver it to my house sometime in the morning. I'll read it at home. You never know. Maybe I'll find something."

"I could have researched all that using the computer."

"Yes, I know, but I want the actual file. What you call the hard copy. I want to see all the handwritten notes, the corrections and the deletions. It helps me form a more complete picture."

Vledder looked searchingly at his mentor.

"And what about me?"

DeKok pushed his lower lip forward.

"Oh, I have something special for you. This afternoon I want you to go back to Utrecht. I'd like you to contact Anton's Marie." He raised a cautioning finger. "Of course, Anton needn't be aware of your call. I don't think she'll talk freely while her boyfriend is around. I have a feeling our petite brunette can tell us quite a bit about Mr. Brassel and the gang."

Vledder looked crestfallen.

"That won't be easy."

DeKok's eyebrows vibrated in that inimitable manner.

"Does it have to be easy?" he asked innocently.

"No, not really, but how will I get her alone? I've the impression that Anton guards her like a hen guards her chicks."

DeKok laughed.

"You come up with some crazy comparisons."

Vledder growled something unintelligible.

"Oh yes," called DeKok after him, "since you're in Utrecht anyway, call two-seven-one-double two-eight. It's a local number."

8

It was almost seven o'clock.

DeKok had been able to sleep until one in the afternoon. Then he had dressed and taken a short walk with his faithful dog, a boxer with a worried and wrinkled face that considered his boss as personal property whenever he was home. Some people said the dog looked like DeKok, and others said that DeKok looked like the dog. Either way, people were right. There was an amazing resemblance between dog and owner.

DeKok had received the files on Jan Brets from Utrecht. He had used the rest of the afternoon to read them. It had been an exhausting task. Brets's criminal feats had moved dozens of civil servants to compose stacks of prose. It was about six thirty when the elder inspector had finally wrestled his way through the mountain of paperwork. Now he was back in the office, more than a full hour before his appointment with Vledder. He decided to take a little stroll through the neighborhood.

The neighborhood, in DeKok's mind, consisted of the famous or infamous (depending on one's point of view) Red Light District of Old Amsterdam. The district encompassed a veritable labyrinth of narrow streets. There were small canals, quaint old bridges, dark alleys, unexpected squares, and architectural wonders. Enlivening the district night and day were exotic, often beautiful women, well-dressed pimps, and innumerable bars and eating establishments. The population swelled with endless streams of the sexually addicted and busloads of tourists from all over the world. For centuries, seamen of every nationality mixed with the locals of the quarter to create an atmosphere that could not be duplicated anywhere else in the world.

DeKok knew almost everybody who resided in the quarter; that is to say, almost everybody in the quarter knew him. He was neither feared nor notorious. He was simply accepted as another facet. He represented the law, but it was just another component of an exquisite mélange.

DeKok was actually well regarded in his district. The pimps and the whores treated him with respect. They knew he administered the law with an even hand. They knew he interpreted the dozens of regulations and guidelines with some latitude. He did not violate the spirit of the law, however he had a unique vision of the letter of the law. DeKok was, indeed, one of a kind, a buccaneer among policemen.

He wore an old felt hat on the back of his head. The belt around his raincoat resembled a worn, twisted rope. DeKok had a broad grin on his face as he strolled past old houses and older canals. Here and there he nodded at acquaintances or familiar faces. They always smiled back or greeted him cheerfully.

At the corner of Barn Alley, he furtively slipped into Little Lowee's small bar. Little Lowee, a diminutive man with a narrow chest and a mousy face, owned a bar frequented by pimps and prostitutes. Little Lowee considered himself a particular friend of Inspector DeKok.

It was still early, and there were only a few customers in the bar. DeKok looked around. He spotted Annie, Cross-eyed Bert's girlfriend. She had already drunk too much. DeKok estimated the intensity of the quarrel that would surely ensue. He grinned to himself. It would probably end up with a fight. Those two had lived like a cat and a dog for years. But neither seemed able to stay away from the other for more than a few days.

He ambled toward the bar and hoisted himself slowly onto a stool. It was his regular seat. From here he could oversee the entire room and his back was covered in case of unexpected eventualities.

Little Lowee approached with a wide smile on his face.

"How's da crime bizniz?" he asked pleasantly. It was almost a stock question.

"Up three points," growled DeKok as if he were quoting the Dow Jones. "It's a bullish market," he added.

Little Lowee laughed.

"Same recipe?"

Without waiting for the answer, Lowee reached under the counter and produced an excellent bottle of Napoleon cognac, a bottle he reserved exclusively for DeKok.

After the usual ceremony—Lowee always drank a glass with him—DeKok leaned back against the wall. He idly wondered why he had given up smoking. It had been more than twenty years, but he still longed for a good cigar while he listened to the piquant conversations between the whores and the other denizens of Lowee's.

It was amazing what they talked about when off duty. Their business was seldom, if ever, a topic of conversation.

It was quiet right now. Just Annie to provide a little entertainment. She sang as she walked from one table to another. It was a sad song, maybe autobiographical, in the meanest Amsterdam dialect. Loosely translated, it was all about a naive girl who threw away her innocence for ten euros. She sang it with a surprisingly good voice.

Little Lowee leaned confidentially over the bar.

"What about da stiff in da Greenland Arms?" he whispered. "Anything to do wiv' youse?"

DeKok took another sip from his drink and nodded imperceptibly. Lowee sometimes acted as an informer, but only for DeKok. It was on a need-to-know basis, and nobody else needed to know about it.

"It was somes guy from Utrecht. Some of da boys 'ere knowed 'im."

"Who?"

"Well, youse know, some of da guys dat hang around. I thinks they knows 'im from inside."

Grinning, DeKok nodded.

"Have you heard anything," he asked carefully, "about plans for a major job in the city? I mean any talk on the street about a big haul?"

Lowee shook his small head.

"Nah, nuttin'. I ain't heard nuttin'."

DeKok looked at him for a long time. His eyes seemed to want to read the thoughts behind the small forehead. Lowee avoided his gaze.

"No?" asked DeKok.

A nervous tic developed on Little Lowee's cheek.

"Should I have?" he asked sullenly.

DeKok smiled.

"No, no, you shouldn't have. It's just a bit strange."

"Strange?"

DeKok sighed.

"Yes, Lowee, I can't help but wonder. If it was such a big deal, why bring a guy all the way from Utrecht? Don't we have professional thieves in Amsterdam?"

Lowee nodded emphatically.

"I should say so," he said, pride in his city evident in the tone of voice. He had momentarily lost his underworld accent. "We don't need them guys from Utrecht for nothing." He picked up the bottle. "Another one, DeKok?"

DeKok nodded thoughtfully.

"Listen, Lowee," he said after a while. "Say someone did recruit a guy from Utrecht for a job in Amsterdam, what does that mean to you?"

Lowee pulled a face.

"It would stink!"

DeKok emptied his second glass and slid off the bar stool.

"My dear Lowee," he said in parting, "you're right. Something reeks."

With that clarification in his mind and two cognacs glowing softly in his stomach, DeKok left the small bar and walked back in the direction of the station house.

He stopped at the corner of Warmoes Street and looked at his watch. It was half past seven. He had plenty of time.

But it was the time that tortured him, because he had no idea what to do next. There was no rhyme or reason in the investigation of Jan Brets's murder. DeKok knew he would have to wait for whatever revelations would come in order to unravel the facts in this perplexing matter. He'd begun to think of it as the Case of the Dead Harlequin. The harlequin was vital to the case. It was inconceivable that a killer would arrange the corpse in that particular position for no reason. It had to be symbolic, or was meant to send a message. He could not think of a single explanation. Again he felt he'd stepped into the absurd. He knew better than to take this personally. However this felt like a practical joke designed for DeKok. The joke was so sinister, he refused to believe that it was only a joke.

He pushed his dilapidated little hat farther back on his head and looked around. About thirty yards away the blue lamp with the word *politie* glowed in front of the police station. He did not feel like returning. Vledder would not have arrived yet anyway.

Crowds of tourists shuffled past him. They came from the direction of the more respectable tourist attractions such as the Rijks Museum, with its magnificent collection of Rembrandts. Now that it was getting dark, people would begin to converge on the Red Light District. During the summer especially, the old neighborhood seemed to be Europe's main attraction. A cacophony of voices engulfed him in as many languages as in Babel. DeKok looked pensively at the throng. He suddenly remembered that Jan Brets, too, had spent three days in Amsterdam before he met his untimely end. What had he done during those three days? How had he passed the time? Did he meet anyone...was he there to meet someone in particular?

He mentally chased the questions. He waited a little longer, and then abruptly turned around. He went looking for Handy Henkie.

Handy Henkie was an ex-burglar. Henkie, a consummate professional, suffered a sudden attack of remorse. For no apparent reason he left his criminal pursuits to follow the narrow path of respectability. He rarely slipped. Henkie considered DeKok to be the greatest influence in his redemption. As a token of gratitude, and to remove a source of temptation, Henkie presented his instruments to DeKok. Henkie, first and foremost a master machinist, had invented and modified tools for his burglary trade. DeKok had to practice long and hard to use them. Sometimes, when absolutely necessary, DeKok would utilize Henkie's tools and talents. On those rare occasions, neither Henkie nor the tools failed him.

DeKok breathed deeply. He laboriously hoisted his two hundred pounds up the narrow, creaking stairs. He hoped Henkie would be home. The mere idea that he might have climbed to the fourth floor on a fool's errand affected his mood. He was already asking himself if he had not been too impulsive. Perhaps he should have asked Henkie to come to the office?

When his breathing was more or less under control, he knocked and entered simultaneously. Henkie, slippers on his feet, was watching television. His mouth opened in surprise when he recognized his visitor. A tic developed along his jaw. He seemed struck speechless.

DeKok walked over to the TV and calmly pulled the plug out of the wall socket. The image of a talking man faded into a black screen. The echo of the voice remained momentarily in the room.

The inspector smiled pleasantly at Henkie.

"Pardon, but I'd hate to have the television distract us, it's so rare I come calling," he said. He paused, then continued. "By the way, good evening."

Henkie swallowed.

"Good evening, Inspector."

DeKok nodded encouragingly.

"Good evening, Henkie."

He lowered himself into an easy chair, placed his old hat on the floor next to him, unbuttoned the top buttons of his raincoat, and stretched his legs comfortably in front of him. Meanwhile, he looked at Handy Henkie, who nervously pulled on his shirt. DeKok enjoyed the confusion of his host.

"I suddenly felt the need to pay you a visit," he started cheerily. "I haven't seen you for some time, and I wondered…"

"You wondered what?"

There was suspicion in Henkie's voice.

DeKok made a gesture.

"I wondered how you were. You see, that's all it was. I was just concerned."

Henkie laughed. It was a strange, nervous laugh. At the same time his sharp eyes anxiously explored DeKok's face. He knew that face. It had become familiar over the

years, from many conversations and even more interroga-
tions. DeKok hadn't changed much. He still had the deep
furrows on his brow and his trademark eyebrows. He had
the same friendly gray eyes and laugh lines around the
mouth. One never knew whether DeKok's mouth said
what DeKok meant.

"I'm all right."

DeKok grinned.

"I can see that, I can see that. You're in better shape
than Jan Brets."

It hit a nerve. Henkie reacted vehemently.

"That's a rotten thing to say," he cried out. "A stinking, rotten thing to say. Jan Brets is dead. I hadda find
out from the paper."

DeKok nodded slowly.

"Yes," he admitted with a sigh, "Brets is dead.
Somebody bashed his skull all to pieces."

Henkie moved in his chair.

"So, what's it to me?"

"That's one of the things I wonder about."

Henkie grinned without mirth.

"That's what you came here for?"

"Yes."

"Now yer pullin' my leg!"

"I mean it."

Suddenly Henkie rose from his chair and gestured
wildly, like a pitchman trying to sell snake oil. There was
a hint of fear in his eyes.

"But, DeKok," he yelled desperately, "you an' me
goes way back! You know I ain't that way... I can't even
kill no fly, let alone some guy like Brets. I might 'a done

wrong, but I ain't no murderer!" Henkie looked utterly miserable.

DeKok looked at him unemotionally.

"Sit down," he commanded. "Did I say you committed murder?"

"Geez, you scared me," Henkie answered, licking his dry lips. "You talk about murder as if it ain't nothing."

DeKok leaned slightly forward.

"Did you know Brets?"

"Yes."

"How?"

"We was both in custody in Haarlem a few years back. He usta walk with me in the yard. He was a safecracker, but he was in for armed robbery, aggravated robbery. He was a violent son of a bitch. Brets wouldn't stop at nothing."

"Even murder?"

Henkie nodded assent.

"Yep. He'd do it, if there was something in it for 'im. He was real anti-...anti- somethin' or other."

"Antisocial," supplied DeKok without thinking. He rubbed the back of his hand over his face. Then he asked, "What did he want from you?"

"From me?"

"Yes."

"Notta damn thing."

"But he was here this week."

Henkie's eyes narrowed. He thought at top speed. Wondered whether DeKok knew or was guessing. It could be a bluff.

"Whaddya mean he was here?" he said finally.

"He came to visit, correct?"

Again Henkie flicked his tongue along his dry lips.

"Jan Brets ain't been here."

DeKok sighed demonstratively.

"Listen to me, Henkie," he said pleasantly, patiently. "You know I have a weak spot for you, but if I were you, I wouldn't count too much on that. These are the circumstances: when we found Brets in his hotel room, we also found a bag of tools. There were some pretty unique items in the bag. Only an expert could design and use those tools. Right away I figured you'd been a busy boy. We know you saw Brets, understand?"

Henkie bowed his head.

"Jesus. I mean, geez," he said sadly. "You ain't never gonna leave me alone." Even Henkie knew DeKok's opinion of strong language.

DeKok grinned.

"So, he was here?"

"Yes."

"What for?"

Henkie stared in front of him and did not answer. There was a melancholy look on his face.

"I didn't go back, you know," he said after a long pause. "Maybe you think I did?" It sounded somber. "I just made some stuff for him, a few tools is all. It ain't against the law!"

"Burglary tools?"

Henkie made a wild gesture. "Wadda ya want from me? It ain't against the law. You could close all the hardware stores tomorrow if it were that. You can get a crowbar anywheres."

DeKok laughed.

"So Brets just came for tools?"

"No, he wanted me in."

"In what?"

Henkie grimaced.

"Something big. He was in a, eh, an organized group. You know, they was like them gangsters in the States, or the Limeys. They had a brain at the top who figured all the angles."

"So?"

"Oh, yes. They coulda used me, he said." Henkie made a nonchalant gesture. "I got experience, know-how and things."

DeKok nodded.

"And?"

"What 'and'?"

"Did you join?"

Henkie's face was the picture of indignation.

"Didn't I promise you back then?" he answered, offended to the deepest part of his so recently reformed soul. "I did promise you I'd quit, didn't I? Anyway, I just don't feel like it no more. I gotta good job now, regular pay." He pointed around the room. "Just lookit, nice furniture, TV, good stuff, and all legit. I never made so much back then…if I did, I'd be too scared to spend it."

DeKok laughed.

"So, Jan Brets talked about an organization. Did he tell you anything else, for instance, who was the leader? I assume that Brets trusted you?"

Handy Henkie nodded emphatically.

"Oh, sure he did. He trusted me. Didn't he ask me to join up? He trusted me awright. The boss, he said, was a counter."

"An accountant," corrected DeKok.

"Yeah, right, an accountant. You know, one of them fat cats lookin' after the cash for them big companies. Guy like that knows where the big loot is. The boys only had to go and pick it up." He pursed his lips and his eyes sparkled. "It sounded real good, yessir, it did. It sounded real good."

DeKok looked at him searchingly.

"But Jan Brets is dead," he said callously. "So how good could it be?"

Henkie nodded a bit vaguely.

"Jan Brets is dead," he repeated somberly. He made the sign of the cross. "God rest his soul."

They remained silent.

"Tell me something about the timing. When was this venture supposed to take place?" asked DeKok. "I mean, had they already finished the job?"

Henkie shook his head.

"Nah, they was still planning, so to speak. They was doin' the job soon, he said."

"When?" asked DeKok, greedy for information. "And where?"

Again Henkie shook his head.

"He didn't say."

"Why not?"

"Crap, that ain't hard to figure out. C'mon, gimme credit. I coulda did it myself. Suppose I wanted their haul? They woulda come up empty handed."

He grinned at the thought.

DeKok rubbed his hand along his chin.

"But," he persisted, "Jan Brets must have told you something about the job. After all, he tried to get you to join them."

Henkie shrugged his shoulders in supreme indifference.

"Not how or where, if that's what you mean. They had a name for it. A code name, you know?"

"A code name?"

Henkie nodded.

"Operation Harlequin."

"What?"

"Operation Harlequin. Crazy name, ain't it?"

DeKok swallowed.

9

Much to his surprise, DeKok found his commissaris waiting for him in the detective room. The man seldom interfered with his cases. Therefore, DeKok found it difficult to suppress an expression of amazement when he found his boss, and Vledder, seated in front of his desk.

"Good evening, Commissaris."

The police chief rose from his chair.

"Good evening, DeKok. Vledder told me that you would be here at eight." He looked at his watch. "It's almost nine now. Anyway, since I was around, I wanted to talk to you about the Brets case. Of course, I've read your preliminary reports, but the summaries were a little too succinct for my liking. I would like more particulars. The press won't leave me alone. Apparently someone got wind the murder was committed under, let's say, unusual circumstances. Now speculation and wild theories are out of control. I think the concierge at the Greenland Arms may have said too much. Further, I'm curious to hear your plans in regard to Pierre Brassel. What are you going to do about him?"

"Nothing."

The commissaris looked at him, thunderstruck.

"Nothing?"

"That's right."

"But, DeKok," exclaimed the commissaris, confounded, "that man, Pierre Brassel, maintains—or maintained—regular contact with the killer. Surely that's obvious."

Slowly DeKok divested himself of his hat and raincoat. He did not feel like discussing the case with the commissaris. It made no sense, in fact it only complicated matters. He would much rather proceed on his own. But as a good subordinate, he had certain duties.

"It may be obvious," he said slowly, "but as far as I know, it's not against the law to merely know a killer."

The commissaris sighed.

"That's not the issue," he said, slightly irritated. "What I mean is, through Brassel you can find the real killer. I just discussed it with Vledder, and I was disappointed you let Brassel go, just like that." The commissaris snapped his fingers.

DeKok shrugged his shoulders.

"What should I have done?"

"D-done?" stuttered the commissaris. "You should have had him followed."

DeKok grinned. Vledder watched carefully. Not even the commissaris seemed immune to that irresistible grin.

"Sir, it would have been a waste of time and personnel. Pierre Brassel isn't psychotic, although his letter might lead one to believe otherwise. He conceived the entire plan in order to keep the actual killer out of harm's way. Brassel voluntarily acts as a red herring. His sole aim was to draw our attention. It's no more than a ruse. One does not have to be clairvoyant to see that."

The commissaris swallowed.

"The last was not a nice remark, DeKok," he said sternly.

Embarrassed, DeKok bent his head.

"Sorry, sir," he answered quickly. "I really didn't mean to be sarcastic. With all due respect, it is clear that shadowing Pierre Brassel is likely to be unproductive."

Again the commissaris sighed deeply.

"All right," he said resignedly, "all right. I'll leave things to you, shall I? In any case, I would like a detailed report on my desk tomorrow. You know how persistent the press can be. It would give me an idea how much, if anything, I can tell them. I certainly don't want your investigations hampered by premature speculation in the press."

"Thank you," said DeKok.

The commissaris had no desire to linger. He said his good-byes and left the detective room.

Vledder sighed. "I really couldn't help it," he said apologetically. "Really, it wasn't my fault. When I got here at eight, I met the commissaris in the corridor. I had to follow him to his office, at once. He kept asking all sorts of questions and was extremely interested in Pierre Brassel."

DeKok nodded.

"Most understandable," he said. "After all, it is a strange business, and he is the chief. He has every right to know."

He paused.

"Mind if I change the subject to something completely different? What happened in Utrecht?"

Young Vledder shook his head sadly.

"I don't think," he said soberly, "my trip was an unqualified success."

Amused, DeKok looked down on him.

"No success at all?"

"I followed Fat Anton and Marie for hours. It was torture. He never left her side for a moment. Happily Fat Anton isn't all that smart, or he would have noticed me several times." Thoughtfully he stared at nothing at all. Then he continued. "Strangely enough, Marie spotted me almost at once. But she didn't say a thing to Anton. If she did, I certainly wasn't aware of it. Finally I decided to pass her a note."

DeKok's eyebrows rippled briefly.

"A note?"

"Yes, in some bar. Anton had gone to the bathroom. I wrote a quick note, asking her to come here tonight, without Anton, obviously. I managed to pass it to her before Anton returned."

Vledder made a helpless gesture.

"I know it's a gamble. If she shows it to Anton, it's all over. But I didn't know what else to do, and I had to contact her somehow."

DeKok nodded encouragingly.

"Under the circumstances, it was the best you could do, probably the only thing you could do. We'll just have to wait. Possess your soul in patience, my boy."

"*What?*"

DeKok smiled.

"Possess your soul in patience. My mother used to say that when there wasn't a thing you could do about something. She meant you just had to wait. A saying, that's all.

A bit old-fashioned, maybe, but it is apt." He scratched behind his ear. "What about the phone number?"

"Nothing, no answer. I tried several times."

DeKok nodded.

"We'll figure it out tomorrow. Utrecht information should be able to tell us whose number it is. Maybe we can approach it from that angle."

The phone rang at that moment.

"This is the desk," said the voice of Corporal Bisterman. "A Marie Sailmaker for you."

"Is she alone?"

"Yes."

DeKok winked at Vledder.

"Wonderful. Please have Marie come up."

After a soft knock on the door, Marie entered the detective room with decisive steps. Her steps were a bit too firm for her elegant high-heeled evening shoes. It created a comic impression, like a longshoreman wearing stilettos. She approached DeKok purposefully.

"You wanted me?"

She was not quite as small as she had seemed next to the enormous thighs of Fat Anton. She had a very attractive figure, and she knew it. Her beige coat closed tightly around her slim physique. A large fur collar covered the bottom half of her face. Her breathing was visible by the movement of the hair in the long fur, like a soft breeze over wheat. She took off a glove and placed Vledder's wrinkled note on the desk.

"Well," she challenged, "here I am."

DeKok gave her one of his sweetest smiles.

"My name is DeKok," he said pleasantly, "DeKok with a kay-oh-kay. This is my invaluable colleague, Vledder. I don't remember having been introduced to you last night." Still smiling, he offered his hand.

She shook it in a businesslike fashion.

"I'm Marie Sailmaker."

"How young are you?"

She chirped like a schoolgirl.

"Guess."

"Twenty," lied DeKok.

She made a movement as if to pirouette.

"You can add five to that."

DeKok forced an expression in which amazement and admiration seemed to battle for supremacy. He gestured toward the chair next to his desk.

"Please sit down," he said with old-world charm and a slight bow. "We wanted to have a serious conversation with you and therefore we used, I fear, an unorthodox method of contacting you. Do forgive me." He seated himself behind the desk and continued. "You see, last evening my colleague and I both had the impression you are an intelligent woman. We felt you would probably be upset if misfortune—or worse—were to befall your friend Anton. It isn't at all impossible that Anton, too, could be..." He did not complete the sentence, but gauged her reaction.

Marie opened the collar of her coat a little. Her sparkling green eyes explored the face of the old inspector. She weighed the value of his words. She was no longer so self-assured. There was a battle going on within her. She obviously had trouble reconciling her natural aversion to and suspicion of the police with the need to protect Anton. She decided she could trust the friendly, fatherly face of the man behind the desk. DeKok noticed the inner turmoil with interest.

"Does Anton know you're here?"

"No."

"You didn't show him the note?"

"No."

"Why not?"

She did not answer at once. She changed position in the chair and pulled her skirt lower over her knees.

"Anton is an ass."

"An ass?" asked DeKok.

"Yes, an ass," she repeated sharply. "A big, fat, stupid ass. Don't ask me why I love that mountain of flab, but I do." She paused. "You want to make something out of that?"

Slowly DeKok shook his head.

"Everybody," he said earnestly, "is entitled to love."

She nodded agreement.

"Exactly, that's how it is. Believe me, there is a good heart inside the boy. He's a bit naive." She smiled tenderly. "A big, naive, good-hearted man. That's him. There's no malice in him."

Her face took on a happy glow. "He's childlike, a darling."

DeKok sighed.

"If we keep this up," he said dryly, "I'll be wondering how our little cherub got lost here on Earth with us common mortals."

She looked confused.

"*What?*"

DeKok grinned.

"I mean, let's not exaggerate. Anton isn't so sweet he wouldn't be part of a gang. After all, he was, or still is, a gang member. Love hasn't blinded you so much you believe Anton has no base impulses."

Her green eyes spat fire.

"If so, it's because of Jan Brets, the bastard. He made Anton crazy. Brets was full of stories: they'd be rolling in money without taking risks. Poor Anton swallowed it all. His ears glowed while Brets spoke. Anton cannot, or will not, think for himself. He's happy to let someone else lead him. Jan Brets was all too happy to lead Anton by the nose."

She pressed her lips together and paused a long time before she continued.

"Clever Jan Brets, with all his jokes and big plans, he's dead. Somebody beat me to it. Otherwise I would have fed him some rat poison one day." She rummaged in her purse and took out a cigarette. She lit up. Her hands shook. She blew smoke toward the ceiling.

"Of course, it's stupid," she said in an even voice, "to say something like that to the police. But you'd have found out eventually how I felt about Jan Brets."

DeKok nodded.

"It's very clear to me," he said laconically. He looked at her for a moment. Then he asked, "When did you first hear about the accountant?"

Pensively she chewed her lower lip. In an indefinable way, it made her look more attractive. Some of the hardness had left her face.

"About two weeks ago. That's when Brets first mentioned his name, Pierre Brassel. Usually he referred to him as his little gold mine."

"Gold mine?"

She nodded, crushed out her cigarette.

"Yes, Jan Brets referred to the accountant that way. Look," she explained, "an accountant deals with a lot of big businesses. He knows exactly how much cash they have, where they keep it, how it is protected...everything. He was going to feed information to Jan Brets. Jan and his recruits, including Anton, would go in and clean up."

"A nice plan."

"Yes, sir. You can see why my Anton was so keen."

DeKok nodded.

"How many times did you meet Brassel?"

Thinking, she placed a long finger alongside her nose.

"Just once. It was evening, about a week ago. Brets brought him to Anton's house, to discuss their venture," she snorted derisively.

"And you were there?"

"Yes."

"You heard what they discussed?"

"Yes."

Slowly DeKok rose from his chair and started to pace up and down the room. He wanted to give her time to realize what she was doing. Experience had taught him it was counterproductive to press people too hard. Circumstances change. People regret and recant what they have said. He placed himself diagonally behind her.

"You do know Anton didn't want to tell us the location of the first burglary?" he asked.

"I know."

DeKok continued, "If Anton finds out you talked to the police, you could find yourself in a world of trouble."

She nodded, almost imperceptibly.

DeKok sighed deeply.

"Very well, then, Marie. What does Operation Harlequin mean?"

She turned in her chair and faced him.

"Will you keep Anton out of this? The only reason I'm here is to keep him out of trouble."

DeKok looked at her unemotionally.

"Has anything happened yet?"

She worried nervously with a glove in her lap.

"No, sir," she said, shaking her head. "Nothing has happened yet. But believe me, sir, I've been scared stiff all this time. Jan Brets was ready to do it! I promise you, he would have. He was going to kill an old night watchman with a hockey stick."

10

DeKok could not control an exclamation of surprise.

"You're certain he was going to use a hockey stick?"

Marie nodded in confirmation.

"That's what he was going to use, a hockey stick. It was one of Brassel's ideas. According to him, nobody would notice a young man walking around with a hockey stick. People go to and come from hockey games, especially on Sunday nights in winter."

DeKok rubbed his hands over his lips. Marie's revelations had him reeling. The veil around the dead harlequin was getting larger and less penetrable, like London fog. Jan Brets planned to kill a watchman with a hockey stick. In an ironic turn of events, Brets's murderer beat him to death with a hockey stick. The odds against a coincidence in the choice of weapons was staggering. Lurking in the fog, like an evil shadow, was Pierre Brassel.

He sat down again behind his desk and pulled thoughtfully on his lower lip. He let it plop back with a most annoying sound.

"To recapitulate," he said, "Brassel, Brets, and the others planned to execute Operation Harlequin on a Sunday night. The obstacle was a watchman, or guard. The plan was to kill him with a hockey stick."

"Yes."

"Excellent. And where was this to take place?"

She made a helpless gesture.

"I don't know if I remember correctly," she said hesitatingly. "I didn't want them to get suspicious, so I tried not to pay much attention. It seems to me it was Bunsum & Company, or Bunsum, Incorporated, something like that. The place is on Drain Street, maybe—yes, Drain Street. There's an alleyway on the corner. Is that possible?"

DeKok nodded.

"That's possible, yes, quite possible. I know which company you mean. It's definitely Bunsum."

She let out a sigh of relief.

"I thought I'd forgotten."

DeKok smiled.

"You didn't happen to overhear which Sunday this was to take place?"

She gestured toward a calendar on the wall.

"Now, this coming Sunday. Jan had gone ahead to look the place over. They needed details about the outside of the building, you know. Brassel was going to give Brets details regarding the inside of the building."

"Do you know what they were after?"

"No."

"Apart from Anton and Jan, were any others involved?"

She gave him a tired smile.

"I think so, but I really don't know anymore." It sounded like an apology.

DeKok placed his hand on her arm in a reassuring gesture.

"Marie," he said in a friendly tone of voice, "believe me, you have helped us."

A worried look came over her face.

"And Anton? What about Anton?"

"I have nothing against Anton," he said, placing his hand on his chest, "nor do I need anything from him. We'll make sure the break-in at Bunsum & Company will not succeed. That's all." He raised a cautioning finger. "Here's what I want," he continued in a compelling voice. "You go back to Utrecht and take care of Anton. You said it yourself—Anton likes to have other people think for him. Well, Jan Brets is dead."

It took a while to sink in. Then a spark of understanding lit up her green eyes. The worried look dissipated slowly, and her face was transformed by a look of relief. She laughed.

"You got it! Damned if I won't do the thinking from now on. I mean all of it!"

"That's the spirit," said DeKok with a smile, ignoring her use of expletives.

As soon as Marie had left, DeKok grabbed the telephone and called the desk sergeant.

"I'd like extra surveillance for Bunsum & Company on Drain Street, from now until Monday night. I don't think anything will happen, but I want it covered. There's a plan to break in, and the plan includes killing the guard there, if he's in the way."

"I'll have the necessary personnel assigned."

"Thank you."

DeKok replaced the receiver. Vledder stood next to him, a piece of paper in his hand.

"I have here," he said, all business, "a synopsis, or rather a conclusion, based on the facts as we now know them. Of course, I've added the information from Marie Sailmaker."

DeKok nodded thoughtfully.

"Marie," he sighed. "I hope she can control Fat Anton. She really seems to love that man."

"May I?" interrupted Vledder impatiently. "May I present my update now?"

"Yes, yes." DeKok's thoughts seemed far away.

Vledder cleared his throat.

"All right, then," said Vledder. "Pierre Brassel, respected accountant, obtains confidential information regarding Bunsum & Company. This information presumably includes knowledge regarding a large amount of cash on the premises. What is his next step? He goes to Utrecht and contacts Jan Brets, a known criminal. He proposes Brets empty the safe or, by whatever means, remove the cash and—"

"Jan Brets agrees," completed DeKok. "He thinks it's a great scheme. He's actually flattered to have the kind Mr. Brassel pick him. After all, any number of underworld characters could as easily eliminate an innocent old man and do the job. Jan Brets immediately contacts his nearest and dearest, settling on Fat Anton. Anton likes the idea as well. Together the brain and the brawn wait for further orders from Brassel.

"Brassel, in turn, orders Brets to take lodgings in the Greenland Arms. From the hotel, Brets will be closer

to the scene. He'll have an opportunity to check out
the lay of the land. Although they haven't agreed on all
the details, the tentative date for the robbery is set: this
coming Sunday."

DeKok made a grand gesture.

"There you are, then," he said, faking enthusiasm.
"It's a neat package; everything falls into place. What we
have here is an everyday criminal conspiracy to drain the
cash from Bunsum & Company."

Vledder shook his head emphatically.

"No, DeKok. I didn't say it's at all logical," he
objected. "Not at all. To continue, even before the
burglary can come to fruition, Pierre Brassel writes you
an idiotic letter. He allows Brets, who has been elected
to do the actual robbery...allows Brets to be murdered
in his hotel room." He snorted audibly. "DeKok, where's
the logic in that?"

DeKok nodded.

"Yes, indeed, Dick," he agreed pleasantly. "If we put
it all together, it is anything but logical. If..." He did not
complete his thought. He stopped and rubbed his hands
through his hair.

Vledder looked at him with surprise.

"If what?"

With a deep sigh, DeKok rose from his chair and
placed a fatherly hand on the young man's shoulder.

"As we discussed earlier," he chided, "take care with
intelligent people. The patterns we design, they've
already inspected and rejected."

"What's that supposed to mean?"

DeKok shook his head.

"Nothing, it's nothing at all. Just take it at face value. Take care not to jump to conclusions. Don't be blinded by what seems to be true at this moment. The most obvious answer is not necessarily the right answer."

"What do you mean?" Vledder seemed totally mystified.

"Let's give it a rest for now," DeKok answered a bit impatiently. "I propose we first get a few hours' sleep. I don't know how you feel, but I'm bone tired." He thought for a while, then said, "Best you go to Bunsum & Company tomorrow morning. You won't rest anyway until you've spoken personally to the manager. You could inquire, tactfully, how much cash they keep on the premises. If possible, offer him a friendly hint to change accountants. We'll see each other again, here in the office, at about noon. Please be sure you bring the watchman with you."

"Bunsum's night watchman?"

"Yes, I want to talk to him."

"Why?"

DeKok was becoming visibly upset.

"Because," he blurted out angrily, "I want to know what in blazes is going on!"

They put their coats on and walked down the long corridor to the stairs. DeKok felt his feet starting to hurt. It was a bad sign, he knew. His feet always hurt when a case did not progress satisfactorily. With some difficulty, he stumbled down the stairs. Vledder was walking in front of him. Outside, in front of the station, DeKok called him back.

"In a little while," he remarked nonchalantly, "if you happen to have a few spare minutes before going to sleep…"

"Yes?"

"I would like you to think about an interesting question."

Vledder looked at his mentor absentmindedly.

"Question?"

DeKok nodded.

"Yes, *why* was Jan Brets murdered?"

A bit lost, DeKok ambled through Utrecht. He felt like a fish out of water. He did not like to leave Amsterdam. He preferred to operate where he knew every street, every alley, and every canal. Utrecht was strange territory. All he really knew about Utrecht was that it contained the tallest cathedral in the Netherlands. He looked around. The canals, he found, did not compare favorably to the canals in Amsterdam. The bridges were too high, the windows too low. It was almost like a foreign country, he thought bitterly.

His old felt hat sat on the back of his head, his reliable raincoat rested on one arm. He ambled along, reading street signs. Feeling strangely isolated, he finally reached Servet Street. Cynthia Worden, a woman who knew Jan Brets, lived on Servet Street. DeKok had her phone number, 271228. He idly wondered what sort of a woman she was. Jan Brets called her twice from the Greenland Arms. Was he her lover?

Servet Street was a narrow passage. It crept along the shadow of the cathedral, which dominated the skyline. DeKok passed a few small shops and stopped in front of a door embellished with a red plastic sign. Cynthia Worden, he read. Underneath were the words *photographic model*. With his little finger he rubbed the bridge of his nose and with the other hand he rang the doorbell.

There was no response to his ring—no movement, outside or in. He looked at the clock tower. It was almost nine thirty: too early or late to call on a model? What time did beautiful people go to bed? Again he pressed the doorbell, and kept his finger on it. After a while, he placed one ear against the door and listened. He could hear the faint buzz of the doorbell from the inside. Otherwise all was silent.

Carefully DeKok looked around. People on Servet Street were busy, he noticed. Much too busy to pay a lot of attention to a middle-aged man in a ridiculous hat who had a friendly smile on his face and constantly rang someone's doorbell.

He searched his pocket for a small tool from Handy Henkie's instrument emporium. It consisted of a brass tube the size of a pocketknife. The tube encased a number of telescoping, adjustable steel pins and something that looked like the beards of keys. DeKok had gained a certain expertise with the innocent-looking gadget. Shielded by his raincoat, he felt for the lock. It did not take long. Within two minutes the door was open. The hinges squeaked slightly as he pushed the door open.

After he closed the front door, he stood just inside and listened for a while. There was no sound. The squeaking of the door had not elicited a response. Carefully, balancing on his toes, he walked down the hall. It was remarkable to see him float silently, moving his oversized body. From a distance it looked like tele-kinesis or a witch's spell. Following pure impulse, he passed the first door but stopped in front of the second. Softly he tried the handle. It moved. With one hand on the doorknob, he suddenly sensed how Jan Brets had died. It had been a quick death. It must have happened almost immediately after he innocently entered his hotel room. He never saw death approach. His assail-ant waited, ready to strike with the reinforced hockey stick. DeKok grinned silently to himself. Perhaps he was now in the same predicament. He, however, was not unwary. Forewarned is forearmed, he thought. He carefully stepped back, turned the knob, and pushed the door slightly. He pushed just a little too fast. The door flew open wide and slammed against something. Every muscle in DeKok's body tensed. The open door revealed nebulous half-light without form, without color. A sensual perfume wafted toward the open door. That was all.

Slowly his eyes adjusted to the gloom. The room he was in took on shape and dimension. He discovered a wide canopy bed in the center of the room. Gossamer curtains hung down on all sides, enclosing the bed. It was a dream, a symphony of pink spun sugar.

Hesitatingly alert, DeKok slowly stepped into the bedroom. Almost immediately he sensed the overpower-ing presence of a woman. The surrounding scent tingled his skin, stimulating his senses. He walked over to the unmade bed and felt the pillows. The pillows were still warm. Only moments before, somebody had warmed the bed.

The air crackled with electricity. The man or woman who had slept in the bed could not be far away. His sharp gaze roamed around the room. He did not see a hiding place anywhere.

Suddenly he stepped back and smiled.

"I would come out from under the bed," he said pleasantly. "It must be uncomfortable. Also, it's probably dusty."

It took a few seconds. A female head with long blonde mussed hair emerged from underneath the bed. The head turned. The eyes stared at the flat feet of the policeman. With amusement, DeKok observed how the woman's astonishment gradually increased.

"How did you get in, who are you?"

DeKok laughed.

"Those are two questions at once. I never answer more than one question at a time."

She stared at him from her position on the floor.

"What are you doing here?"

DeKok did not answer directly. His mind was busy with something else. He also wondered about the strange perspective from which she was looking at him. It must be a comical sight for her.

"Why don't you," he proposed, "come out from under the bed. That way we can continue the conversation at a more normal level."

She sighed audibly.

"You will have to leave a moment. I'm not dressed."

DeKok made a decision.

"Just tell me where your clothes are. I'll hand them to you and I'll turn around while you put them on."

He saw her hesitate.

"I promise," he said with a winning smile. "Believe me, that still means something to men of my age."

She stretched a slender arm toward a low bench in front of a dressing table.

"My robe."

DeKok picked up the desired article of clothing and tossed it in her direction. Then he turned his back discreetly. A few seconds later she walked by him on bare feet. She was a good- looking woman, no taller than shoulder height on a man like DeKok.

"Come into the living room," she said. Her voice was devoid of any kind of accent.

She walked down the corridor in front of him. DeKok followed complacently. Meanwhile, he admired her supple figure. Although giving the appearance of ethereal fragility, she was not skinny as models often are. On the contrary, her figure seemed pleasantly filled in all the right places.

In contrast to the bedroom, the living room was drenched in daylight. The sheer window curtains formed the only barrier between the room's interior and the outside world. The décor was tastefully modern. Modern paintings, in bizarre color combinations, managed to impart a cheerful atmosphere.

Cynthia Worden curled up like a cat in a sort of hammock on legs and gestured DeKok toward a wide bench without armrests. She seemed completely at ease. DeKok gazed at her searchingly, looking for signs of age or stress, but could not find any. The daylight didn't compromise her beauty.

"How did you get in?"

"I rang," answered DeKok.

She nodded.

"I heard that. You are, how shall I say it? You are rather tenacious."

"When you didn't answer, I came in. Your front door," he lied, "was not locked." He ignored her astonished gaze. "Perhaps I should introduce myself," he continued. "My name is DeKok, with a kay-oh-kay. I'm a police inspector from Amsterdam. I've been assigned the investigation regarding the death of Jan Brets."

He saw the shock go through her. Her alluring pose was immediately forgotten.

"You're from Homicide?"

The corners of her mouth trembled. She stood up from her hammock and grabbed a pack of cigarettes. Changing her mind, she threw the pack down again and fiddled with a cigarette lighter. She lost her composure.

"What do you want from me?"

Her voice sounded scared.

"Just a bit of information, is all," said DeKok. "For instance, who was the victim to you? What was your relationship?"

"Well, there was no question of an affair."

"Tell me what to call it."

"What?"

"Your relationship with Jan Brets."

She sat down again in the hammock, very chaste, the robe tight around her knees.

"We were friends."

DeKok nodded.

"All right," he said. His tone was one of resignation. "You and Brets were friends. Excellent, we're making progress. Therefore I can assume you would mourn his death, isn't that right? After all, that's common, isn't it...among friends and acquaintances?"

She looked sharply at him, trying to gauge whether he was joking. His face showed utter sincerity.

"Well," she said finally, "we weren't really close."

"Yet he called you twice, shortly before his death?"

"Yes."

"Why?"

The corners of her mouth trembled again.

"Just conversations, nothing special."

DeKok pressed his lips together. He did not feel like conducting a long and laborious interrogation. Time was short. He had to be back in Amsterdam by noon.

"Now, you listen to me," he said sternly. "As a rule I couldn't care less about conversations between young men and women. I have an interest in Jan Brets. He is dead. Somebody smashed in his skull, and I want to know who and wherefore, Ms. Worden. You have some explaining to do. Oh, and I would encourage you to explain your comic behavior in hiding under the bed."

She did not answer, but lowered her head. DeKok suddenly noticed she was crying. A few tears dropped on the hands in her lap. DeKok resisted the urge to get up and place a protective arm around her shoulder. He would have liked to do it. But he remained seated, outwardly unmoved. In a very short period he had witnessed too many—too rapid—mood swings. It made him suspicious. He waited patiently for her to dry her tears. When she looked up again he saw that she had cried real tears. He let her be, waited until she spoke of her own accord.

"I'm afraid, Inspector," she said after a long pause. "It seems best to tell you everything. Really, I'm afraid for my life. When you opened the door of my bedroom, I thought you'd find me and kill me."

Her voice was now calm, without emotion. She was no longer posing. Her big blue eyes were serious.

"Is that why you crawled under the bed?"

She nodded.

"I thought it was him!"

"Who?"

"Freddy Blaken." She sighed deeply. "A former boy-friend of mine."

"Well, what about him?"

The expression on her face changed. There was total, unadulterated fear in her beautiful blue eyes. She stretched her arms toward DeKok beseechingly.

"You must catch him!" She uttered this wildly. "You must find him as soon as possible. You must arrest him before he comes back here. He killed Jan Brets!"

11

DeKok raked his fingers through his hair. The wild accusation from Cynthia had not shocked him in the least. He knew from experience not to give her emotional statement much weight. He took all spontaneous allegations with a grain of salt. They were usually the product of suppressed emotions; he needed supporting facts, evidence, or a witness.

He looked at the young model. She sat before him, shivering in her robe, a frightened child. He suddenly recognized her face. With surprise he remembered having seen her hundreds of times, laughing cheerfully from upbeat advertisements on billboards, in the papers, in magazines. He grinned bitterly. The way he saw her now was not an example of exuberance.

"Why don't you put on something warmer," he encouraged. "You don't have to be tempting, beautiful, or provocative for me. I'm just a civil servant with the soul of a petty official." He made a sad gesture, pointing at her. "All that would be wasted on me."

A faint smile brightened her face momentarily.

"Just a moment, then," she said and left the room.

She returned within minutes, dressed in jeans, a thick, formless sweater, and a pair of fuzzy slippers in the shape of rabbits. She had also found time to brush her hair. It framed her face in glorious waves. She was one of those people who could dress in sackcloth and still be striking.

"So," said DeKok when she had seated herself again, "your former boyfriend Freddy Blaken killed Jan Brets?"

"Yes."

"Why?"

She pulled her head between her shoulders.

"He hated Brets. Freddy was jealous of him."

DeKok nodded.

"The same feeling of hate, of jealousy, prompts him to seek your death?"

"Yes."

Thoughtfully DeKok pulled on his lower lip.

"Well," he said with a sigh, "if Freddy's love for you was in proportion to his present hatred, he must have been *very* enamored."

Her eyes locked with his. The tone of mockery in his voice had not escaped her.

"People witnessed the threats," she said sharply. It sounded like a reproach.

"Witnesses?"

"Yes. There are plenty of people who heard Freddy say what he would do. 'First I'll break that clown's skull. Then I'll come after you,' he said."

DeKok sat closer to the edge of the bench. He seemed suddenly very much interested.

"Clown?"

"Yes."

DeKok looked at her with amazement.

"He called Jan Brets a clown?" he asked.

She nodded emphatically.

"Clown, or joker. You see, Freddy couldn't stand Jan being the life of the party…any party. After Jan managed to grab the spotlight, Freddy would curse. He didn't like Jan, said he was a show-off." Her tone of voice changed. "Jan *was* fun. He was a fun guy. That's why I went with him."

DeKok sighed. The eternal triangle, he thought.

"And you left Freddy for that?"

"Yes. Freddy took himself so seriously. I mean moody, gloomy. Finally I couldn't stand it anymore."

"When was the final break?"

She did not answer at once. She finally succumbed and lit up a cigarette. She inhaled deeply, as though she was enjoying her first cigarette after quitting.

"I've been avoiding Freddy the last few days," she said through her wreath of smoke. "I just happened to meet him again recently in a bar. That was the day before yesterday. I told him it was over between us, that I was dating Jan and that he didn't need to come back." She sighed, crushing her cigarette after only a few puffs. "It developed into quite a row."

DeKok nodded.

"He became furious. That's when he said he would kill Jan and you?"

"Yes."

"So this took place on the day someone murdered Jan?"

Her head barely moved in assent.

"Yes. It was the day of the murder," she repeated tonelessly.

They remained silent. Outside, on Servet Street, they heard a car honk and a child yell something.

"His threat makes it appear," said DeKok after a pregnant silence, "that Freddy made good on his promise, as far as Jan Brets is concerned."

He spoke more to himself than to the young woman. He rubbed his hands over his face pensively. His thoughts built an image. He tried to relive what happened in the Greenland Arms.

"How did Freddy know," he asked suddenly, "where to find Jan Brets?"

"How? They were in the syndicate together." There was surprise in her voice.

DeKok's eyebrows rippled briefly.

"What syndicate?"

"Yes, well, they were part of an organization to…" She stopped talking, then went on, "I don't really know if I'm supposed to talk about it."

DeKok looked at her evenly.

"Jan is dead," he said flatly.

"You're right," she agreed, "it doesn't matter anymore." She moved a blonde lock of hair out of her eyes. She made an ordinary gesture elegant. Her blue eyes were moist.

"Someone from Amsterdam," she whispered, "approached Jan. It was evidently a man well-placed in the business world. He asked Jan to build an organization in Utrecht, a syndicate to execute a series of burglaries."

"But why in Utrecht?"

She shrugged her shoulders.

"I think the man said something about Utrecht being centrally located, with a hub of connections and roads, you know? After all, we *are* in the center of the country. Anyway, he thought it would be easier to operate from Utrecht than from Amsterdam or Rotterdam, for instance."

"Go on."

"Jan liked the plan and went in search of partners. He knew Freddy Blaken from before. About two weeks ago he stopped by to ask Freddy if he wanted to join."

"And?"

"Freddy was interested and Jan became a regular visitor."

DeKok sighed.

"With fatal consequences?"

She nodded.

"I liked Jan a lot better than Freddy, almost from the start. He was so much more cheerful. Freddy warned me about Jan, told me to stay away from him. According to Freddy, Jan was dangerous, a brute with at least one murder under his belt." She smiled indulgently. "But Freddy was just jealous."

DeKok nodded slowly.

"And jealous people…" He did not complete the sentence, but asked, "Do you know if the syndicate has actually executed any operations?"

"No, I don't think so. Everything was still in the planning stages."

"Do you know any other participants? Have you ever heard the name Fat Anton?"

Slowly she shook her head.

"I never knew the names of the others."

"The man from Amsterdam, do you know him?"

Again she shook her head.

"I don't know him. Just heard his name once or twice. It was Brasser, Brassel, something like that. I don't know exactly."

DeKok took a deep breath.

"Listen to me, this is important: do you know of any other people who referred to Jan Brets as a clown or a joker?"

She waved her hands vaguely.

"No. Freddy was the only one."

DeKok remained silent for a long time. Then he picked up his hat from the floor and rose slowly to his feet.

"Come on," he ordered, "put on something more suitable. You're coming with me."

Taken aback, she looked at him.

"With you?"

DeKok gestured impatiently around.

"You certainly don't expect me to leave you alone in the house while Freddy walks around, maybe with murder on his agenda?" He shook his head emphatically. "No, my dear girl, it would be out of the question. You're coming to Amsterdam with me. I know of a small, friendly hotel where you can hide out for a while. It's safer for you and better for my peace of mind."

She voiced her objections, but finally agreed to DeKok's request.

As she went to leave the room to pack, DeKok followed up with, "Please keep it modest," he said with small-minded conservatism. "People already look at me strangely."

12

_____

"What's your opinion of Cynthia Worden?" Vledder was
still intent on processing DeKok's report of the events in
Utrecht. His brain tried to assimilate the new information and make it fit with what they already knew. The
new developments, he thought, opened a number of fresh
perspectives. "Can you trust her, you think?" he asked.

DeKok made a helpless gesture.

"What do you mean by trust?" he asked carefully.
"She seemed to me to speak the truth."

"So Freddy Blaken really threatened Brets?"

"Oh yes, no doubt about that. I even assume there
were witnesses who would testify under oath."

Vledder spread out both arms.

"Well," he said impatiently, "what are we waiting for?"

DeKok looked at him, cocking his head to one side.

"What do you want to do?"

"Arrest Blaken, what else?"

"On what grounds?"

"Murder."

"Oh."

Vledder slapped his hands flat on the desk.

"Yes," he cried enthusiastically, "he's the man we're
looking for. Just think: yesterday we couldn't understand

why Brets was murdered. There was no motive. Now we have motive of jealousy. We didn't know why the corpse was placed in that strange harlequin position. Well, here's the explanation. Freddy called Jan a clown, and he posed Jan's dead body like a clown." He looked seriously at his mentor. "It all fits!" he continued. "Freddy Blaken hated Brets so much he wanted to insult him, even in death. That's why he posed him like a harlequin. You see what I mean? He made a statement: Jan Brets, the clown, is dead."

A strange silence fell on the room. The last words of the young inspector echoed around the bare walls. It was as if the death of Brets had become tangible. DeKok pushed his lower lip forward.

"Jan Brets," DeKok said tonelessly, "clown unto death." He looked encouragingly at his protégé. "Clever," he added admiringly, "very clever. It's a great theory. My compliments."

Dick Vledder looked at him, suspicion in his eyes. He listened for a tone of sarcasm in DeKok's voice. There was none. The admiration of his older colleague seemed sincere.

"But it won't be easy," continued DeKok, "to find Freddy Blaken. I asked Cynthia specifically, but she didn't know where he could be. Anyway, she's scared stiff of her former boyfriend. I had to assure her several times she would be safe in the hotel."

"And is she?"

DeKok sighed deeply.

"It seemed the only solution. What else could I do? I could hardly give her a police escort, not with the shortage of personnel. And it just wouldn't do to place her in protective custody. I don't think she belongs in jail. So long as our Cynthia doesn't show herself in the street, the hotel is the safest place for her. I know the owner. He'll keep an eye on her. Of course she isn't registered under her own name. She registered as Mrs. Vledder."

Vledder looked at him, wide-eyed.

"Why Mrs. Vledder?" he asked, irritated.

DeKok shrugged his shoulders.

"What does it matter? I couldn't think of anything else at the time. Anyway, you could do worse for a wife. Cynthia is quite beautiful."

Vledder looked daggers at him.

"Beautiful or not," he growled, "I don't like it. From now on, use your own name for that sort of thing. If Celine discovers there's already a Mrs. Vledder..."

DeKok laughed heartily.

"Aha," he joked, "so, *that's* the problem!"

Vledder snorted.

"There's no problem," he exclaimed, "but I would like to draw your attention to the elderly gentleman who has been waiting for you for more than an hour."

"An old man?"

Vledder nodded.

"The night watchman from Bunsum. He had to be here by noon, you said. Remember?"

DeKok gripped his head with both hands.

The man looked very neat. He wore a brown corduroy suit with leather patches on the elbows. He did not look at all like a night watchman. He looked more like a bohemian, with long, wavy hair and a well-trimmed beard. His brown eyes darted restlessly around.

DeKok apologized sincerely.

"I'm very sorry," he said, "to have kept you waiting so long. You have every right to complain about my behavior. I hate to admit it, but I'd forgotten we were expecting you. It simply slipped my mind. I'm so sorry, please excuse me."

The old man laughed.

"To be truly repentant," he said, "is no shame. It's therefore remarkable how seldom it happens."

DeKok looked closely at the old man. He detected both spirit and education in the voice. It surprised him.

"You're a night watchman?" he asked tentatively.

The old man nodded cheerful assent.

"For Bunsum, on Drain Street."

"How long have you been doing that?"

"About two years. Ever since my wife died." The old man looked sadly in the distance. "It was necessary," he continued. "I simply had to find something to do, or I would have died too. My daughter was right. 'Papa,' she said, 'find something to do. You're just pining away.' She introduced me to the younger Bunsum." He smiled shyly. "That's how I became a night watchman." He paused. "You see," he continued, "it suits me and my daughter very well. When I come home in the morning, I fix her breakfast and call her in time to go to the office. I sleep while she's at work. She sleeps while I'm at work. It's an ideal arrangement. We get along just fine, my daughter and I."

DeKok nodded.

"What was your profession before you became a night watchman?"

The old man pulled his beard while he answered.

"A teacher. I taught industrial arts, mechanical drawing to be exact."

"Oh?"

"Yes, it's a bit different. But I had to retire, you see, at sixty-five. I'm almost seventy now, in just a few more months."

DeKok showed his admiration.

"Well, you certainly don't look it," he said. "You look very fit."

The old man beamed.

"Well, I am. I can still take care of myself."

DeKok nodded slowly. He wondered if the old man was fit enough to fend off a thug wielding a reinforced hockey stick. He did not think so.

"You ever have any problems on the night shift?"

"Oh no. There isn't all that much worth taking, I think. Actually, I'm less of a watchman and more of a handyman. I like to keep busy, so I fix things."

"But the firm finds it necessary to have a guard at night?"

"Yes."

"Do you work Sundays?"

The man nodded emphatically.

"Certainly, quite a few weekends."

"Including this coming Sunday?"

A smile lit up the man's face.

"No," he said, shaking his head, "as it happens, not this coming Sunday."

"You have a replacement?"

Again the man shook his head.

"No, no replacement. This coming Sunday there won't be anyone on duty."

DeKok's eyebrows started one of those amazing dances. The old man watched in fascination.

"No guard?" questioned DeKok. "But…"

"Oh, it doesn't matter, once in a while. Young Bunsum thought the same when I asked him. After all, it would be rather coincidental if something were to happen the one time I'm not there."

DeKok swallowed.

"S-sir," he stuttered, "why won't you be there this Sunday?"

The man's eyes sparkled.

"My daughter and I," he said, "have both been invited to a party."

"A party?" asked DeKok.

He nodded emphatically.

"Yes, my daughter is a secretary for Brassel & Son, CPAs. Her boss, Mr. Brassel, is throwing a party for the staff at his house next Sunday. He invited me as well."

DeKok rubbed his face with both hands. It was an extremely weary gesture. Finally he found his voice again.

"I think," he said tiredly, "I have enough information for the moment, Mr., eh…"

"Petersma," supplied the man.

DeKok smiled politely.

"Mr. Petersma, thank you very much for coming to see me, and once again my sincerest apologies for having kept you waiting."

The old man stood up and walked toward the door.

"Just one more question," called DeKok. "When did you get the invitation to the party?"

He reflected a moment.

"Two weeks ago," said Mr. Petersma.

With his head in his hands, both elbows resting on the desk, DeKok stared into the distance. He was dazed. His usual melancholy expression had turned desolate. He felt himself sinking deeper and deeper into quicksand. His brain worked at top speed. Restlessly it looked for a point of reference, a handhold, a starting point. Vledder took a chair and placed it across from him.

"So, Brassel's lovely secretary, the green-eyed brunette with the irresistible dimple on her cheek, is the daughter of Bunsum's night watchman."

DeKok grinned.

"Exactly the same night watchman who was supposed to be knocked down by Jan Brets during Operation Harlequin. The one for whom the hockey stick was meant."

"But," said Vledder with wonder, "there's something that doesn't compute. There would be no watchman for Brets to knock down."

DeKok nodded slowly.

"You're right, Dick, it doesn't compute. The carefully prepared hockey stick was superfluous. The watchman wasn't going to be there. He's been invited to a party."

Vledder swallowed, a sudden lump in his throat.

"A party at Brassel's."

DeKok stood up and started to pace up and down the detective room. He stopped in front of the window and looked outside.

"It's a comedy of errors," he said wistfully. "A farce for our amusement, if only Jan Brets had not been so thoroughly killed."

He turned toward Vledder.

"You went to Bunsum this morning?"

"Yes."

"Well?"

"Nothing."

"What do you mean, nothing?"

Vledder shrugged his shoulders in a careless gesture.

"Exactly what I'm saying. Mr. Bunsum had no idea what a burglar could find worthwhile in his building. There was nothing to steal, he thought. The big money, the real money, went straight to the bank. There was only a small amount of petty cash in an old safe."

"What about their accountant?"

"It wasn't Brassel."

"No?"

"No."

DeKok's eyebrows were getting a workout. Vledder watched, fascinated. He carefully tried to imitate the movement. As always, he failed.

"But," said DeKok after a long pause, "Brassel's secretary had enough influence with Bunsum & Company to make sure her father would get a job as night watchman."

Vledder nodded.

"Easy enough, if Brassel cooperated."

"How's that?"

Vledder smiled a secret smile.

"They're friends."

"Who?" DeKok sounded impatient.

"Brassel and Bunsum. They were in grade school together."

13

Inspector Vledder thought deeply. His youthful face was serious. His chin stuck out and a deep vertical wrinkle appeared on his forehead. Suddenly his eyes lit up. The chin withdrew and the deep crease disappeared.

"I've got it!" he exclaimed. "It's as clear as day."

DeKok, who was studying a floor plan of the Greenland Arms, looked up, a blank expression on his face.

"What's clear?"

Vledder sat down across from him.

"Why Brassel invited the watchman to his party."

"Oh yes, why then?"

"Easy," smiled Vledder. "He didn't want his secretary's father to come to harm."

Shaking his head, DeKok looked at Vledder.

"I'm certain," he said, "that it's not exactly as simple as you think. Just think for a moment about what Marie Sailmaker told us yesterday. Do you remember how she told us it had been agreed during the planning at Fat Anton's house to do something about the night watchman? Remember how Brets was supposed to take care of that? Brassel supposedly suggested it could best be done with a hockey stick? That was about a week ago! At the time, Brassel already knew there would be no guard on duty. He had invited the guard a week earlier."

Vledder groaned as if in pain.

"Yes," he cried, angry with himself. "You're right. It's true. Petersma had been invited a week earlier, two weeks ago." He stared out the window, chewing his lower lip. He resumed after a moment's hesitation. "But why didn't Brassel say anything? Why would he propose to render the watchman harmless and why would he suggest the hockey stick?"

DeKok raised both arms.

"Yes," he said, exasperated. "Why indeed? Why was Brets killed with the prepared hockey stick?"

At that moment the phone rang. Vledder picked it up.

"No, one moment." He handed the phone to his partner. "It's for you," he added.

"DeKok here."

"I promised to call you," said the voice at the other end of the line, "if anybody took an interest in Mrs. Vledder, the lady you brought over earlier today."

"Yes."

"There was a man here a little while ago."

"And he asked for Mrs. Vledder?"

"No, he didn't ask for Mrs. Vledder, but he meant her. He called her something else."

"What?"

"He called her Cynthia, Cynthia Worden."

DeKok threw the receiver down and went over to the peg to get his coat.

"Come on," he called over his shoulder, "let's hit the road."

"Where to?" asked Vledder, surprised.

DeKok was struggling into his coat on the way to the door.

"Hotel Dupont and Freddy Blaken."

The owner-doorman-waiter-chef of Hotel Dupont quickly dried his hands on a white apron and led the policemen to a seating arrangement in the small lobby.

"It was a good-looking young man," he explained, "black hair, good clothes. He made a bit too much noise, maybe. You know what I mean? The guy was macho, didn't seem to have good manners, he used some vulgarity. I'd guess his age at about twenty-five. He asked to speak to the girl who had checked in this morning. I pretended I didn't understand him and asked him what girl he was talking about. That's when he mentioned the name."

"Cynthia Worden?"

"Yes."

"What next?"

"Nothing. I told him as far as I knew, there was no Cynthia Worden staying here. I didn't lie. Then he left."

DeKok laughed.

"Did he leave a message or did he tell you he would be back?"

"No, he didn't do either. I'm sure he'll be back, though. He seemed surprised not to find her here. He asked if there were any other hotels on Martyrs Canal."

DeKok nodded.

"Where's the girl now?"

"Upstairs, in her room." The hotel owner pointed with his thumb.

The inspectors stood up and walked toward the stairs. Halfway there, DeKok turned around and asked, "Did our little beauty make any telephone calls after I left?"

"No, at least not from here. I have no phones in the rooms, just this one at the desk." The man shook his head. "I would have seen her," he added.

"Did she leave at all?"

"Just for a minute, to get some cigarettes. Maybe a few minutes."

DeKok nodded thoughtfully. He walked a few steps back and stopped in front of the hotel owner, hand on his chin.

"If our visitor returns," he said, groping for words, "while my colleague and I are upstairs, ask him if he means a blonde girl with blue eyes. If he admits that, and I'm sure he will, bring him upstairs. Knock three times in quick succession on the door, wait a few seconds, then open the door and shove him inside. We'll take it from there."

The hotelier nodded.

"What if he doesn't want to come upstairs?" he asked.

"Don't worry, he'll come up."

Beautiful Cynthia was not at all happy to see Vledder and DeKok enter her room. On the contrary, there was a definite expression of disappointment on her attractive face. DeKok gave her a friendly grin.

"We're here to protect you," he said cheerily. "We got a tip that Freddy Blaken has been spotted in the neighborhood. Apparently he's looking for you. He asked for you downstairs not long ago."

She did not react immediately. She appeared unmoved by DeKok's announcement. She darted a furtive glance at the inspectors, but there was no sign of fear.

"We're happy to see you're still alive," continued DeKok in the same cheerful tone. "I gave the owner clear instructions." He paused and sneaked a look at the expression on her face. "Otherwise we might have been *too late!*" He said this in a lugubrious voice.

Her eyes narrowed.

"You're spying on me?" she yelled at him.

DeKok shook his head.

"Not at all, not at all," he answered calmly. "I've just taken some necessary precautions. That's all. Remember, you told me you had no idea where Blaken could be found. How was I to know you would contact your own murderer?"

"I didn't contact him."

DeKok lifted both eyebrows briefly.

"But didn't you phone him this morning to tell him where to find you?"

She avoided DeKok's eyes and lowered her head. Her blonde hair closed off her face as if a curtain had been drawn.

"Didn't you phone?" insisted DeKok.

"Yes."

"Strange behavior for a prospective victim."

She raised her head slowly. The blonde curtain opened up. Her big blue eyes looked at him. They were moist and a tear rolled down her cheek.

"I want to make up with Freddy," she whispered. "You understand, Mr. DeKok, I wanted to make up before it was too late and you'd arrest him." She sighed deeply. "After all," she went on, "he did it all for me, just for me, because he loved me. I only realized that after I had already betrayed him."

DeKok rubbed his face with a flat hand. He looked at her intently between his fingers. He was in uncharted waters. Love and women…he knew it was a combination fraught with quickly changing emotions. He thought briefly about his own wife. He had never been able to discover why she loved him.

"Is that why you asked him to come here?" he asked the girl.

She nodded slowly.

"To talk it over," she said listlessly.

DeKok pushed his hat slightly forward and scratched the back of his neck.

"So you *did* know where to reach him?"

"I only had a phone number, in Utrecht."

DeKok grimaced.

"Weren't you afraid he would hurt you?" He continued, sarcasm in his voice. "Only this morning you crawled underneath the bed just at the thought it might be him."

A sad smile hovered around her lips.

"This morning, yes." She sighed as if a century had passed since then. "I changed my mind; I'm no longer afraid. If you hadn't alerted the man downstairs, Freddy would have come up. I would have had a chance to tell him I still love him. I could have apologized to him for the affair with Jan Brets...could have told him it was nothing but a mistake." She crushed the collar of her dress between nervous fingers. "Then it would have been up to him," she said with another deep sigh.

The expression on Vledder's face was a mixture of painful surprise and embarrassed disbelief.

"You would have just waited for him to react?" he asked incredulously. He snapped his fingers. "Just like that? Kiss me, kick me, or kill me, I don't care!"

As if in a daze she stared past him and nodded.

"You're crazy," he spat vehemently. "Certifiable! That's not love! It has nothing to do with love, it's—"

He was interrupted by three quick knocks on the door. DeKok shoved Vledder to one side and sprang away himself, out of view of anyone entering the room. In the same moment the door flew wide open. A powerfully built young man stood on the threshold. His dark eyes looked into the room.

A moment of paralysis followed, a pause in the action that lasted no longer than a split second. During one heart-stopping instant, Freddy Blaken stood eye-to-eye with his former love and thought about his next move. In that split second, Cynthia screamed.

Her short, sharp scream bounced from one wall to another, alarming Freddy. He felt the threat, then caught the approach of both inspectors in his peripheral vision. Lightning fast, he sprang into action. He whirled around, threw the hotel owner against a wall, and fled down the stairs.

"Grab him!" yelled DeKok.

Vledder bolted out the door.

Freddy Blaken took the stairs in two jumps and raced through the lobby, running out into the street. He threw an old man to the ground and barely escaped an approaching streetcar.

Vledder followed. As soon as he got outside, he saw Blaken turn the corner of the first side street. It was an area regularly patrolled by constables on foot. They're never around when you need one, thought Vledder. The disappointment slowed him down. He panted. His heart throbbed in his throat. His legs felt like lead. His quarry was at least fifty yards ahead of him and the distance seemed to increase. Blaken ran into one street and out another. When he finally took the time to look around, he could not see Vledder anywhere. Reassured, he slowed down. Finally, upon approaching Damrak, he slowed to a walk, mingled with the crowds, and disappeared in the throngs that entered Central Station.

14

"So, he escaped?"

Vledder hung his head in shame.

"That guy ran so much faster than me. He fled via Herring Packer Alley toward Damrak. He must have disappeared in Central Station. He just vanished in the crowd. Evaporated."

DeKok smiled at the frustrated face of his colleague.

"Don't worry about it," he said encouragingly. "We'll get him eventually, if not today, tomorrow. Anyway, I'm not so sure he's the man we want, after all."

Vledder looked at him with surprise.

"You think he's *not* the murderer?"

DeKok shrugged his shoulders.

"I don't know. We would first have to interrogate him at length. You see, the murderer of Brets must satisfy at least one very important condition."

"And that is?"

DeKok made an expansive gesture with both hands.

"He would have to be close to Pierre Brassel. He would have to have been in a position to let Brassel know the murder would happen. You see, the murderer must have told Brassel about his plans...and by yelling over the crowd in some bar, as Cynthia told us. No, it would have had to take place in an atmosphere conducive to planning, no, to *premeditating* a murder. That takes calm, quiet discussion of detail. Cynthia may have flattered herself, believing one of her lovers killed the other over her. The fact is, Brets was not the victim of a crime of passion." He paused and rubbed the bridge of his nose with his little finger. "Blaken seems to have been the only person to call Brets a clown, but it may not be significant," he concluded.

Vledder walked over and leaned on the desk.

"You're still worried about the harlequin posture?"

DeKok nodded. He appeared lost in thought.

"No explanation has surfaced." His voice betrayed his disappointment. "There is a lot in this case for which there seems to be no explanation. Cynthia's allusion to a syndicate is fantastic, not to say illogical. Just think. A group plans to commit burglaries, the first of which is to take place at Bunsum's. Bunsum is a friend of Brassel. Part of the plan is to murder a night watchman, to get him out of the way. Brassel, however, invites the intended victim to a party. Jan Brets is the actual burglar, but he's killed. Brassel doesn't lift a finger to prevent the murder."

Vledder nodded sadly in agreement, but suddenly his eyes lit up, as if a single spark had set off an entire new thought process.

"You're right," he exclaimed, wildly enthusiastic. Vledder's moods could be as mercurial as the weather. DeKok made this silent observation, not for the first time. "It would not be logical," continued Vledder, speaking rapidly, "for Brassel to allow anyone to murder Brets, whom he needed more than anyone else in the so-called gang!"

DeKok, still musing about Vledder's mood swing, gave him a confused look.

"I don't understand you."

Vledder laughed, triumph in his voice.

"You know," he said, raising a finger in a subconscious imitation of one of DeKok's stock gestures, "he didn't need Brets at all for the burglary. There wasn't going to be a burglary."

"Come again?"

Vledder grinned.

"There wasn't going to be a burglary," he repeated. "Nobody could gain anything by breaking into Bunsum & Company. Pierre Brassel was never serious about Operation Harlequin. It wasn't just fantastic, it was a phantasm. The so-called syndicate, or gang, the entire plan, was a masquerade. Brassel made it all up. His only purpose was to get Brets into the Greenland Arms. Brassel set an elaborate trap!"

"A trap?"

Vledder nodded emphatically.

"Brassel enticed Brets to take lodging at the Greenland Arms by pretending he would give Brets inside information for a big money theft and, probably, more to come. Brets fell for it. Believe me, it had to be that way. Brets fell into a trap."

Thoughtfully, DeKok chewed his lower lip.

"Still one question remains: who killed Brets and why?"

Vledder's face fell.

"You're right," he admitted, downcast, "it really doesn't give us anything new."

DeKok placed a fatherly hand on the young man's broad shoulder.

"Wait. It isn't at all an idle thought," he said. "No, not at all, on the contrary." His voice was encouraging. "I really believe that Brets was enticed into a trap. It really looks that way."

Suddenly he looked piqued. He shook his head and walked away from Vledder. He started to pace up and down the room in long strides. It was always easier to think on his feet. An avalanche of questions needed answers. After about ten minutes, he sat down at his desk and took a blank sheet of paper from a drawer. In the upper left-hand corner he wrote the word *trap* in large block letters. He hesitated a moment, pen in hand, and then added a question mark to the word.

It was one of his habits. He had developed these customary behaviors over the years. If something particularly bothered him, he would write it down. He believed he could change the question from something abstract to a concrete manifestation by committing it to paper. He stared at the bare word and tapped his middle finger on the center of the paper.

"How did Brassel know?" he asked, irritation evident in his tone of voice. "How did Brassel, a respectable citizen, a professional man, know of the existence of a man like Brets, a man with a rap sheet like an encyclopedia?"

He looked up at Vledder.

"What interest could a man like Brassel have in a man like Brets that would compel him to murder?" He grinned without mirth, still irritated, and gestured toward the piece of paper. "Was it Pierre Brassel? Did the accountant have anything to gain from Brets's death? It's hardly credible."

They remained silent for a long time. DeKok stared at the word *trap*. Vledder was occupied with his own thoughts.

"It doesn't compute," said Vledder after a while, repeating his earlier statement. "There's just no logical connection anywhere. One thing is obvious, at least at this moment. Brassel is involved up to his tidy chin hairs—no doubt about it! We just cannot fit him into the puzzle, no matter how we try. It really comes down to a single question: what's Brassel's involvement in all this?"

DeKok stood up.

"Let's go ask him," he said.

Vledder looked at him, baffled.

"Ask who?"

DeKok grinned.

"The man who seems to have all the answers."

Vledder beamed.

"Brassel?"

"Yes."

It was a nice, welcoming house, made of red brick with large windows. The area was just outside the suburbs, between the airport and Amsterdam, not far from the main highway, just far enough to give the illusion of country living. Light poured from the windows.

DeKok judged it better to confront the accountant at home rather than in his office. Offices, according to his experience, were impersonal, characterless. They seldom offered a glimpse into the personality of the user. But a home often mirrors the people who live there. That is why he waited until evening.

It was not difficult to find Pierre Brassel. He was, so to speak, on display. The Dutch have a peculiar habit of never closing curtains, except, sometimes, bedroom curtains. Tourists make it a point to walk the streets of Dutch cities, peeking into rooms as they pass by. Nobody takes offense. On the contrary, the Dutch take great pride in their interiors. The interiors invite people to look. Neighborhoods in Dutch cities resemble shopping galleries for furniture and decorating styles. Inhabitants go about their normal occupations, oblivious to the interest of passersby.

Pierre Brassel was sitting in an easy chair in front of the fireplace. He was reading. Farther back in the large room, his wife was seated at a large round table, engaged in embroidery. It was a peaceful scene of domestic tranquility and coziness, bathed in a diffused light that suited the image of a respected accountant at leisure.

Although DeKok, like all the Dutch, seldom gave a particular interior a second thought, he felt a pang of guilt. He always felt guilty peeking into the home of someone connected to a case. It gave the police an unfair advantage, he thought. His puritanical background tended to trip him up on these occasions. He felt that he was intruding on the intimacy of the two people in the house, catching them in the act. He would, however, excuse his actions, citing the national habit of putting homes on display. Sometimes, thought DeKok, I am too complicated for my own good.

He and Vledder viewed the tableau for some time, under the cover of darkness. The domestic scene at Brassel's home made the notion of criminality, especially murder, appear ludicrous. DeKok could not help but think of it all as a bizarre joke. Anytime now, he thought, somebody would start laughing. It might come from the bushes, loud and wholehearted laughter waking up the quiet complacency of the street. All the neighbors would come out to laugh at him, DeKok, the crazy inspector from Amsterdam. He suspected their respected, admired neighbor of nefarious activities. He sighed deeply, then he touched Vledder's arm and approached the door. He hesitated for one more moment. Then he rang the bell.

They did not have to wait long. A handsome, slender woman opened the door. The voluptuous lines of her figure were silhouetted, etched sharply against the light from within the house. The light sparkled in her blonde hair. DeKok wondered for a moment if he had ever met her before, but he could not place her. Then he thought cynically that his path, at times, seemed to be literally strewn with beautiful blonde women. But of course, there were a lot of beautiful blonde women in Holland, and a lot of them looked alike.

"Mrs. Brassel?" he asked, lifting his hat politely.

She nodded calmly.

DeKok gave her his most winning smile.

"DeKok, DeKok with, eh, a kay-oh-kay."

She offered her hand in a friendly manner.

"I've heard a lot about you," she said simply.

She had a slight German accent. It sounded pleasant, the way she spoke.

"This is my colleague Vledder."

"How do you do."

The greetings and introductions were conducted in a formal manner. Mrs. Brassel did not seem the least bit surprised by the visit from the two policemen. She acted guileless and natural, as if the men had kept a long-planned appointment.

"You wish to speak to my husband?"

DeKok nodded and took his hat in his hand.

"Yes, ma'am, that is the purpose of our visit."

She pointed at a coatrack in the hall.

The long-legged Brassel was the epitome of a cheerful host. He arranged easy chairs in a half circle, placed a few small tables within easy reach, and beamed with forthcoming friendliness.

"Coffee?"

Vledder and DeKok nodded ready assent.

Brassel motioned to his wife and she went to the kitchen. DeKok looked after her admiringly until Brassel again required his attention.

"I read somewhere," remarked the accountant airily, "the police in general, and especially the Amsterdam police, consider coffee to be one of life's elixirs. One of the tools needed to do the job. Is that right?"

DeKok smiled politely.

"Yes, you might say that. It's a tonic, all right, a well of inspiration. Although some people need stronger stimulants for inspiration."

Brassel did not react. He gestured toward the waiting chairs.

"But do sit down, gentlemen," he said with easy urbanity. "My wife will be here with the coffee in a moment and you'll be able to judge how coffee *should* taste. She's of German origin, you know, my wife, and a marvel in the kitchen. People who have eaten at our table always wonder how I manage to stay so slim." He grinned apologetically. "But apparently, I don't have a tendency to, eh…"

DeKok looked at him mockingly.

"A tendency to what?"

Momentarily, something flashed in Pierre's eyes. Then his lips curled into a smile.

"Corpulence," he declared.

DeKok grinned.

"That's nice."

Brassel stretched his long legs and leaned comfortably back in his chair. He placed the tips of his fingers against each other.

"The John Bull type doesn't happen in our family," he continued. "I can indulge myself with my wife's culinary offerings and it will have no effect on me."

Vledder changed position in his chair. The meaningless chatter irritated him in great measure. He preferred to get to the point. His impatient temperament did not like beating around the bush.

"Have you wondered at all," he asked, "why we're here?"

Pierre Brassel absentmindedly looked at the inspector, as if annoyed by the interruption.

"Excuse me?"

A blush appeared on Vledder's face. The unspoken rebuke irritated him even more. He pulled himself forward to the edge of the chair.

"Do you know why we're here?" he repeated.

Pierre Brassel nodded calmly, unperturbed.

"It seems rather obvious," he punctuated this remark with a sigh. "You have a problem with the rather sudden death of Jan Brets in the Greenland Arms. I refer to a professional problem, of course. It isn't difficult to imagine you're very upset about it. It seems your investigations in the case have been rather fruitless up to the present. You have no starting point, too few connecting links, and so on. Because of my little letter and, of course, my visit to the police station, you believe I can name the murderer." His tone of voice was strictly businesslike, as if he were discussing the implications of a profit-and-loss statement. "Isn't that right?" he asked in conclusion.

Vledder caught his breath.

"Right, that's it," he uttered. "That's exactly it."

DeKok enjoyed himself silently. He smiled behind his hand. The face of an astonished Vledder was positively comical to watch.

Mrs. Brassel entered and served coffee. She had also changed. She now wore a simple gown of black material that contrasted alluringly with her clear ivory-colored skin. She also served a slice of homemade cake, which elicited a compliment from DeKok.

"Wonderful," he cried out, enchanted. "Extremely fine.

I've never tasted anything like it. My wife should have this recipe."

She gave him a sweet smile.

"I'll get it to her," she almost whispered, "before the week is out."

The secretive tone made DeKok look up in surprise. His eyebrows rippled briefly.

"Before the week is out?" he asked.

Pierre Brassel hastily intervened.

"It's a matter of tradition," he said, a little too loudly and emphatically. "My wife is from a very old German family. The special recipes in the family have been handed down from mother to daughter."

DeKok nodded his admiration.

"A fine tradition," he said, "worth maintaining."

Mrs. Brassel smiled dejectedly.

"There are other traditions in our family—" She stopped suddenly. There was a warning in her husband's eyes. A warning that did not escape DeKok. He looked at her with new interest.

"What sort of traditions, Mrs. Brassel?"

She glanced at her husband and sighed.

"I was referring to less-innocent traditions."

Brassel laughed, but his eyes contained no humor.

"I'm sure my wife refers to a few common traditions, farmers' traditions, at least from the Middle Ages. Isn't that so, Liselotte?"

She lowered her head and nodded.

Brassel immediately turned the conversation in a different direction. In some way he was afraid of what his wife might say. Whenever she spoke, he watched her anxiously, followed every word with singular intensity. It was obvious he preferred to keep the initiative himself. He turned toward DeKok.

"You have," he asked, "found no mistakes on the part of the murderer during your investigations?" His tone was politely interested.

DeKok shrugged his shoulders.

"That's difficult to answer," he replied thoughtfully. "I'm sure there were mistakes in the murder of Jan Brets. I don't believe in the perfect crime. However, I must admit we haven't discovered any mistakes yet."

Brassel beamed, obviously pleased with himself.

"But that doesn't mean a thing," added Vledder hastily. "Just because we haven't found any mistakes doesn't mean that no mistakes were made."

The accountant shook his head and laughed. It was an insulting, contemptuous laugh. Again he stretched his long, thin fingers and placed the tips against each other.

"You two," he said with a condescending arrogance, "have a strange way of reasoning. Every form of logic is missing from your statements." He gestured vaguely. "Mistakes," he explained further, "are only mistakes if they are discovered. They simply do not exist before that. They are born at the moment of discovery. Undiscovered mistakes have no reality." He paused and grinned. "I hope the gentlemen follow me?" he asked gratuitously.

DeKok pressed his lips together. Brassel's supercilious manner was getting on his nerves.

"For my part," he said grimly, "there is but one reality: the murder of Jan Brets." He stretched an arm in the general direction of the complacent accountant. "Speaking of logic, perhaps you could explain something to me. Why would an intelligent man, a respectable citizen with a charming wife and two young children, be so willing to gamble with twenty years of his life?"

Brassel snorted.

"What are you talking about? Twenty years?"

DeKok gave him a penetrating look.

"The penalty for murder," he said curtly.

Brassel reacted vehemently.

"Twenty years for murder? In Holland?" He laughed insultingly. "Ridiculous, and you know it! No judge in the country will hand down a sentence of twenty years, even for the murder of a whole village." He paused and took a deep breath. Calmer, he continued, "In any event, *I* haven't committed any murder."

DeKok grinned broadly.

"Ah, but there's such a thing as complicity. You could be judged an accomplice before, during, or *after* the fact."

Brassel stood up abruptly.

"Accomplice? *Accomplice?*" He took a few long steps toward the bookcase. His normally pale face was red with emotion. "Here!" he exclaimed, pointing at a row of neatly bound books with gold letters on the spines. "Here, I have the complete criminal code and all relevant jurisprudence for the last one hundred years. I have carefully worked my way through it. I promise you, I know it word for word. I've taken advice from the best legal minds in the country." He stretched a finger in DeKok's direction. "If you can prove my complicity in regard to the murder of Jan Brets, you're a lot smarter than all the lawyers, prosecutors, and judges of this century."

Unimpressed, DeKok shrugged his shoulders.

"I'm not a judge, a prosecutor, or a lawyer," he remarked mildly. "I'm just a simple cop. I don't have to prove your complicity. If I only have a simple suspicion, I've enough to arrest you." He grimaced. "Of course, the justification for such an arrest is a matter for later discussion."

Pierre Brassel was getting visibly upset.

"I know the limits of your authority," Brassel said in a shrill voice. "You cannot arrest me! You can do nothing against me. You haven't the right." Goaded by DeKok's mocking smile, he went on, "You accuse me of being a murderer and you speak of justice?" He shook his head in disgust.

"Mr. Brassel," DeKok spoke slowly and with a threatening undertone to his voice. "You would do well to remember one thing. You're able to play this amusing little murder game with me because you rely on my honesty and my trustworthiness as a guardian of the law. I must say, it's especially flattering. Yes, indeed, my goodwill stands between you and incarceration."

Brassel looked at DeKok with suspicion.

"I don't understand," he said softly. "Your honesty… my freedom?"

DeKok nodded emphatically.

"If you had read the law correctly, you would have known you were obligated to warn Jan Brets, one way or the other, that he was about to be murdered."

Brassel smiled a superior smile.

"But I have done so," he said, self-assured. "I wrote him a note. You probably found it under the corpse."

DeKok looked at him with feigned surprise.

"A note?"

"Yes. I wrote a warning note."

DeKok's face showed only dismay.

"I found no note," he lied. "None of us has seen a note like that."

Brassel looked at him, disbelief in his eyes.

"But you must have."

DeKok made a helpless gesture.

"Sorry," he apologized. "There was no note. I fear this so-called note exists only in your imagination. Therefore we have no choice but to conclude you failed to warn Brets when you knew his life was in danger. You leave me no choice. You committed a criminal offense."

For the first time, Brassel lost his temper. He stood in front of DeKok and looked down at him. His hands shook. Bright red spots bloomed on his cheeks.

"You did find it," he screamed. "You must have found it," he repeated with special emphasis. He spoke slowly, like a teacher in front of particularly stupid students. His voice thundered through the room. DeKok remained seated, unmoved. He thoughtfully rubbed the bridge of his nose with a little finger and looked up at the man in front of his chair.

"What's the matter, Mr. Brassel?" he asked, sarcasm dripping from his voice. "Aren't you feeling well?"

Pierre Brassel gestured wildly, waving his arms.

"That's low," he spat angrily. "It is a false, mean, underhanded lie. You have the note. Of course you have the note. You found it under the Brets's body. I wrote it and Fre—" He stopped suddenly, swallowed the last word as a horrified look appeared on his face.

The red spots of anger disappeared. All color drained from the man's face. He looked pale as a ghost. Mrs. Brassel, too, was thoroughly shocked. But she recovered faster than her husband.

"I believe I understand, Mr. DeKok," she said softly. "You're just trying to scare my husband, aren't you? You did find the note of which he speaks?" She spoke in a sweet tone, as if beseeching him. "You just want to let him know that you *could* have said the police found no note and my husband gave no warning." She sighed deeply. "You meant you *could* say that if you were a dishonest person."

The door opened at that moment and a darling little girl of about six entered hesitantly. She wore light blue pajamas. Long ringlets of blonde hair spiraled from her head to her shoulders. She rubbed the sleep from her eyes with tiny fists.

"*Ich kann nicht schlafen,*" she said softly, whining in German. "*Soviel Schall.*"

Mrs. Brassel sprang up, went to the child, and led her out of the room with softly soothing words.

This brief interruption gave Brassel the opportunity to regain his composure. He sat down again and the color slowly came back to his face. He rubbed his forehead with the back of his hand.

"The poor child must have been wakened by the noise," he said with a sigh. "But then, you *did* give me a scare."

DeKok ignored the remark.

"Your daughter?" he asked.

Brassel shook his head.

"No," he answered, "little Ingrid isn't my daughter. She's my niece, the youngest daughter of my wife's brother. She's just staying with us for a visit. She's a rather nervous child. Very sensitive to surroundings, people around her." He gave a tired smile. "My own children are different, less vulnerable. They sleep through anything, even an earthquake."

Mrs. Brassel returned after a few minutes. She held an index finger in front of her lips, a recognizable gesture in any country.

"Ingrid's asleep again," she said. "Please, let's be less noisy. The child is such a light sleeper."

She turned toward DeKok.

"The problem of the missing warning note has meanwhile been resolved, I hope?"

DeKok nodded.

"Indeed, I did find it," he answered with a smile. "It was underneath the corpse, as your husband guessed."

She breathed a sigh of relief.

"In that case, would you like another cup of coffee?"

Vledder and DeKok nodded in unison.

"What about you, Pierre?"

Brassel looked up, momentarily lost in thought.

"What?"

"Coffee?"

"Coffee? Yes, yes, all right."

DeKok grinned.

"Absentminded, Mr. Brassel? Where were your thoughts? On a pitch?"

Brassel looked at him, incomprehension on his face. "Pitch?"

"Yes, the pitch, the field. After all, it isn't all that long ago you were the captain of your university's field hockey team, was it?" DeKok scratched his ear with an embarrassed gesture. "You were especially recognized for your hit work, your stick technique, I believe." He grinned his irresistible schoolboy grin. "Or do I have the terms wrong? I know little about field hockey."

15

Vledder guided their trusty old VW Beetle back to Amsterdam, keeping his speed at under forty miles per hour. They drove along the Amstel River; the dam on the Amstel was the origin of the name *Amsterdam*. The river was wide, much wider than normal. Water splashed up on the road. A sharp, howling wind created whitecaps on the dark water. It was somehow sinister. More so, reflected Vledder, when one realized the surface of the river was several feet below sea level. On a night like this, only the dikes, the sand dunes, and the ubiquitous windmills stood between Holland and impending disaster. Dark clouds chased one another along the sky, blotting out the moonlight. Silhouetted against the dark sky, a lone farmhouse took on a ghostly appearance.

DeKok paid no attention to his surroundings. He did not see the clouds or the rain. Windmills all over the country were turning madly under reefed sails, keeping water tables at manageable levels. DeKok remained completely detached. He did not care whether Vledder had trouble distinguishing between roadway and river surface. He sat low in the passenger seat, almost on his shoulder blades, his hat deep over his eyes. He yawned with obvious pleasure.

"I'm sleepy," he allowed between two huge yawns. "Let's stop a moment at the station, just in case. Then we'll go home."

Vledder nodded slowly, his eyes glued to the road. The beam of one headlight on the VW wasn't straight and gave him less visibility than he would have liked. On the other hand, it did allow him to keep a weary eye on the wild water of the river. As they approached the city, the driving became a little less stressful.

"I have a feeling," said Vledder, "there's another murder in the offing."

DeKok groaned from underneath his hat.

"One murder is enough for now, thank you very much. Just try to control your feelings."

Vledder laughed.

"Was Pierre Brassel really a hockey player?"

"Yep, a good one too, so I've been told."

"And the stick, I mean the hockey stick that killed Brets, was that one from Brassel's personal collection?"

DeKok nodded, but Vledder did not allow his eyes to stray from the road. DeKok said, "Yes, it belonged to Brassel. The lab found traces of the initials *PB* in the wood. Apparently it was done years ago, with a pencil. It had worn down, of course, but it was still detectable with the right instruments. No results on the tape or the lead, yet. I understand there's little to go on. Perhaps they can find out where it came from, but to tell you the truth, it seems not to be very important."

Vledder sighed deeply, stretching to relieve his cramped muscles.

"I don't understand it at all." He was piqued, sounding almost like a spoiled child. "We've nothing but why—why this, why that," he continued. "One thing's for sure: Brassel's playing with fire. Were it not for a cast-iron alibi, he would have been locked up long ago. He could very likely have been convicted of the murder of Brets. Just think of all the evidence we could have presented." He smiled bitterly. "But all that evidence is for naught. We were with him when the murder was committed. We can hardly move the time of death to suit the prosecution."

DeKok laughed and pushed his little hat back on his head. He raised himself in the seat with difficulty.

"Here's the thing, Dick," said the gray sleuth, looking for words, "the ridiculous letter he wrote, the one asking for an appointment, had only one purpose. It was to provide him with an airtight alibi for a murder he knew was going to be committed. He helped plan a killing, of that I'm convinced." He turned in his seat, faced Vledder. "You see, my boy," he continued, "it's especially the last part I don't understand. It bothers me the most."

"How's that?"

"Well you see…" He stopped, raised a finger in front of his eyes, and stared at it, as if he had never seen it before. "Brassel apparently participated in the preparations *voluntarily*! Certainly he had no objections. He didn't try to stop the killer, no, he extended a helping hand." Again he paused. "Why does one commit murder, particularly a carefully premeditated murder? Why help the murderer prepare to kill the victim?" DeKok found a use for the finger in front of his face, he added the rest of his fingers and counted on his outspread hand "Greed, vengeance, jealousy, fear, blackmail."

He lowered his hand, glanced disinterestedly out the window, and shook his head.

"As far as I can determine," he continued his soliloquy, "none of those motives would have driven Brassel. Think about it. Brets was a crook, but a broke crook. He was still living with his mother. We saw for ourselves it was anything but luxurious. Nothing is known about any Brets/Brassel contact in the past. They didn't know each other before Brassel sought out Brets for the alleged break-in at Bunsum. Somehow we must see all this as related to the act of preparing for murder. The real motive is not connected to any of it. It has to do with something that happened before."

They were in front of a red light, so Vledder darted a quick glance aside, his face beaming.

"Excellent, very good," he cried enthusiastically. Neither man noticed Vledder was using one of DeKok's stock phrases. "You have something there. Nobody has to teach you how to suck eggs, no sir. That was a clear, concise explanation, completely logical." The light turned green. He grinned while he engaged the clutch. "Your performance at the Brassel home was also a classic, by the way. That little white lie about not finding the note shook him to his core."

DeKok smiled at the memory.

"Yes," he admitted, "our Pierre lost his cool for a while. In a way, I was surprised. I would have thought him a lot stronger."

"What do you mean?"

DeKok sighed.

"I thought he was less vulnerable."

Vledder nodded.

"What do you think? Will we be able to charge him with something, when the time comes?"

"I hope not."

"*What?*"

DeKok shook his head.

"No, really," he said, his face serious. "I mean it. I hope we will never have to charge him with any specific crime. I wouldn't like that at all. I would sincerely regret it. I found him a thoroughly sympathetic man."

It was a good thing they were in the city, partially sheltered from the gale-force weather. Utterly shocked, Vledder almost lost control of the car.

"Brassel," he chided, "*sympathetic?* We are talking about the same arrogant, supercilious citizen who consistently ridicules us? Are you cracked? If Brassel's little game ever becomes common knowledge, you can kiss your reputation good-bye."

DeKok shrugged his shoulders.

"Ach," he responded with a wan smile, "my reputation can stand the occasional mud bath. That's the least of my worries; it's not important what people think."

He rubbed his face with both hands.

"You see, I actually pitied Brassel tonight. I watched him very carefully. There was more fear than bluster. The apparently oh-so-superior Mr. Brassel is scared stiff something may have gone wrong. He's not so sure of himself. Despite his careful preparations, even studying the relevant statutes, he's afraid we can charge him with something. Just think about his vehement behavior when I spoke of complicity."

Vledder nodded.

"You're right. But I don't think that's reason to find him sympathetic."

He guided the battered VW around the monument on the dam, aiming it for Warmoes Street. He stopped in front of the entrance to the station house.

The desk sergeant gave them a long-suffering look when Vledder and DeKok appeared in his line of sight.

"There you are, finally," he called. "Where were you two?"

DeKok looked at him. His eyes questioned the speaker.

"What's been happening?"

"I tried to reach you everywhere. Your car radio must be on the blink again, or did you turn it off? Anyway, I've had a guy here for the last few hours and I don't know what to do with him."

"What guy?"

"One Freddy Blaken. He came in to give himself up."

DeKok assessed the young man's appearance. Then he pointed at a chair next to his desk.

"Won't you sit down?" he invited. "To what do we owe the pleasure of your visit?"

Freddy Blaken looked suspiciously at the gray sleuth.

"Pleasure? Ain't I wanted?"

DeKok gave him a friendly grin.

"Let's just chat for a while. For instance, about your friend Jan Brets and his untimely demise. You apparently had no time for us this afternoon. You seemed rushed."

The man nodded slowly.

"I shouldn't have run," he sighed. It sounded sincere. "That was dumb, real dumb. I figured it out later. That's why I came to give myself up. I'm trying to make up for the bad impression you might have of me. I didn't kill Jan Brets."

DeKok grimaced, a look of utter astonishment on his face.

"But didn't you say, in the presence of witnesses, I might add, you were going to bash in his skull?"

Freddy lowered his head and nodded.

"Yes, I did," he admitted tonelessly, "but—"

"Here's my problem," interrupted DeKok,. "After you made the threat, a few hours later someone murdered Brets by splitting his skull. Don't you think the coincidence is remarkable?"

Blaken shook his head.

"I didn't do it," he said simply.

DeKok ignored the remark.

"Ach," he said, gesturing grandly, "it's fairy tale time, is it? Well there are other coincidences. Let me enumerate."

Blaken jumped out of his chair.

"You don't get it," he cried emphatically, "I didn't do it."

DeKok placed a surprisingly strong hand on the shoulder of the young man and gently, but irresistibly, forced him back on the chair.

"You will listen," he said severely, "to what I have to say, Mr. Blaken. I could have had you arrested this afternoon. And not just because you took off in such a hurry!"

The man swallowed. His Adam's apple bobbed up and down.

"Go ahead," he said softly. "Please," he added as an afterthought.

DeKok rubbed his hands through his hair, as if to gather his thoughts. Vledder generally vacillated between amusement and irritation over DeKok's theatrics.

"There were, Mr. Blaken, only a few people who knew Jan Brets was staying at the Greenland Arms. You were one of the few. You were a member of a so-called syndicate. You knew Brets was in Amsterdam to prepare the way, so to speak. Once you became furious with Brets, you knew exactly where to find him." He made a vague gesture while he let the words sink in. Then he added, "We know you were in a murderous fury when you threatened to crush skulls. None of it bodes well for you. You threatened, you had opportunity, and you had a motive for murder."

Blaken looked up, shocked and scared.

"Motive?"

DeKok nodded with special emphasis.

"Jealousy. You were envious of Brets because of his interest in Cynthia, which she seemed to reciprocate. Jealousy, Mr. Blaken, is a powerful motive for murder." He paused. "And another thing, young sir, the murderer placed Brets's corpse in a position that closely resembled a harlequin. Apparently you were the only one to call Jan Brets a clown and a joker." DeKok pushed his lower lip forward. His tone became sarcastic. "All things

considered, what do *you* think your chances would be
in front of a judge?"

Again Blaken shook his head vigorously.

"I didn't do it," he exclaimed. "It's all false, false, false."

DeKok sighed.

"How long have you known Pierre Brassel?"

"Brassel?"

"Yes."

"I *don't* know him."

DeKok looked at him intently. A dangerous fire
sparkled in his eyes.

"You must know him."

Blaken hid his face in his hands.

"I don't know him. I don't know him." There was
despair in the voice.

"Didn't Brets introduce you?"

"No, I never met Brassel. Jan told me about him.
That's true. He was supposed to be the man behind the
scenes, the organizer, the tipster."

DeKok nodded.

"When was Operation Harlequin scheduled for
execution?"

Blaken looked at him with a stupid look on his face.

"Operation Harlequin?"

"Yes."

"Hey...I don't know. I never heard of no Operation
Harlequin."

"Then," cried DeKok in exasperation, "what would
Brassel need *you* for?"

"He needed my connections in case he needed a fence.
Look, I have relations, people who buy things without

asking questions. Jan knew it, he used to send me his 'excess inventory.'" In that moment Freddie's expression made him look like a faithful basset hound. "If I was ever interested in other people's business, it was long ago. People trust me *not* to ask questions. In my business, curiosity can be fatal, in more ways than one. See no evil…hear no evil…speak no evil."

DeKok smiled just thinking about it.

"Nevertheless," he tried, "Jan Brets did visit you regularly."

Freddy displayed a sad grin.

"He didn't come to see me. Not for business, that is. He came for Cynthia. The bastard. He knew we'd been engaged for two years, knew we planned to marry." He paused, shrugged his shoulders. "Nobody should wish anybody dead, even an enemy. But Jan Brets deserved what he got, in fact, he asked for it. Maybe the killer did me a favor, but I don't know who it was. It had to happen sooner or later."

DeKok nodded. He rose from his chair and walked over to the peg in the wall and grabbed his raincoat.

"Come on," he tossed over his shoulder, "let's go."

Vledder looked at him in surprise.

"What about him?" He glanced at Freddy.

DeKok nodded.

"Put on your coat and hold on to Freddy."

They abandoned the detective room and walked down the dark old corridor to the stairs. They said good-bye to the desk sergeant on the way out. Before long they were on Damrak. Damrak connects Dam Square to

Station Square, in front of Central Station. DeKok halted abruptly in the middle of the deserted street.

"Take Freddy to Hotel Dupont," he ordered. "Tell the owner it's all right."

"What about you?"

DeKok gave him a tired smile.

"I'm going home. I'll walk. I need the fresh air."

He waved farewell and disappeared in the rain.

Vledder and Blaken stared after him.

They saw him shuffle along the other side of the street, his raincoat tight around his large body, his little felt hat tipped far forward. He looked like a drunken reject from the bar scene, refused his last drink.

He did not turn around.

16

An agitated DeKok paced up and down the large detective room. His face gave away a stormy, foul mood. It was nine o'clock and there was no coffee. The culprit was the new, very young Detective Bonmeyer. According to the duty roster, the boy was supposed to have taken care of the coffee that morning. He was too inexperienced to know an early burglary and interrogation were not his first priorities. In DeKok's eyes, this was simply unpardonable. Nothing could be more important than the first coffee of the morning. He read poor Bonmeyer the riot act in the choicest possible terms. DeKok took the youngster to the window, pointing to the Royal Palace. Should the palace be burning, Bonmeyer's job was to first make coffee. Regardless of what might be going on, DeKok *expected* his coffee to be ready.

Right in the middle of another thunderous expression of dissatisfaction, the phone rang. DeKok leapt toward it, grabbed it, and yelled into the receiver.

His tone changed almost immediately when he learned who was on the other end of the line.

"Good morning, Mrs. Brassel, what can I do for you? An appointment? Yes, of course…this morning, at ten? Most certainly. Where would you like to meet? Here?

Ah, if not at the station, where do you suggest? What's that you said? Yes, the restaurant in Amstel Station? Yes, I know where that is, no problem. Until then, good day, Mrs. Brassel."

Gently he replaced the receiver and scratched his neck. What did the handsome Mrs. Brassel want? Why did she insist upon meeting on neutral ground? A commuter railroad station in the suburbs was not the ideal place for an assignation of any sort. He immediately rejected the possibility that she had fallen head over heels in love with him. That was simply too absurd. Even his wife, a model of indulgence, had taken years to get used to his looks. In the end, she couldn't resist him or his friendly boxer. No, he reflected with a sigh, it would be business, just business. Anyway, they would have fresh coffee in the restaurant.

He closed his desk drawer, threw one more devastating look in the direction of the hapless Bonmeyer, pulled on his coat, and left the room, still sulking.

Downstairs he met the commissaris, entering as he was leaving. DeKok quickly pulled up the collar of his coat in a forlorn attempt to hide and tried to escape via the rear entrance. He was doomed to failure.

"DeKok!"

Slowly DeKok turned around, forced a friendly grin on his face, and approached his chief reluctantly.

"Good morning, sir."

The commissaris lifted his hat.

"Good morning, DeKok," he said cheerfully. "Come with me a moment, would you?"

DeKok rubbed his chin.

"I, eh, I have an appointment at ten," he protested.

The commissars looked at his watch.

"Oh," he laughed, "plenty of time."

He climbed the stairs with remarkable agility for a man of his advanced years. A little slower, DeKok followed him.

The commissaris threw his briefcase on a table. Still with his coat on, he sat down behind the desk and stretched an arm toward DeKok.

"Give me your report," he said. His tone was serious. "We'll have time to go over it together."

DeKok swallowed.

"Report? What report?"

The commissaris frowned.

"I do believe," he said, irritation in his voice, "we agreed. Either you or Vledder was to give me a detailed report regarding the happenings at the Greenland Arms."

DeKok bowed his head.

"You are absolutely correct, sir," he said with feigned deference. "We did agree. However, I do not yet have a report for you. We've not had time. In any event, we have no details to report. Jan Brets was knocked down with a reinforced hockey stick. That was all there was in the preliminary report Vledder wrote." He shrugged his shoulders. "We have found little to add," he concluded.

Angrily, the commissaris rose from his chair.

"I want a *detailed* report."

DeKok made an apologetic gesture.

"I don't have it."

"Then you prepare it, at once!"

"I have an appointment."

The commissaris was getting red in the face.

"I want," he yelled furiously, "a detailed report *today!* You understand? I want a detailed report about the Brets case. From you! I don't care how! Today!"

DeKok was already in a foul mood because of the coffee. With difficulty he suppressed a number of less suitable observations. Instead he bit his lip and sighed deeply. In an obsequious tone he asked whether the commissaris had any other orders.

Yes, the commissaris did. It seemed the management of the Greenland Arms kept phoning him to ask whether housekeeping could remove the seals from room twenty-one. It had been almost two days. They were losing money.

DeKok could not contain himself any longer.

"What a load of horse crap!" he exploded. "Less than forty-eight hours ago a man was savagely murdered in his hotel room! Now the hotel management is whining about a sealed room. My management is whining about a report. Maybe we should call Parliament into session!"

The commissaris showed an almost imperceptible smile on his face. DeKok must be really upset to use a vulgar reference to manure. It was the strongest language he had ever heard DeKok use. He had known DeKok a long time, trusted him, and was prepared to put up with his peculiarities.

"Go away, DeKok," he said wearily.

DeKok left.

The coffee in the Amstel Station restaurant went a long way toward reconciling DeKok to his fate. He'd already had a bad day. If it progressed the way it started, he could forget it. He reflected philosophically on the life of a cop: down today, up the next. Sometimes it was a blessing not to know what was going to happen next.

He thought about the interview with his chief and the detailed report. He grinned to himself. Who solves a murder by writing a report? The clock was ticking and he wasn't wasting his time. The commissaris should know better. He ordered a second cup of coffee and waited patiently for Brassel's wife to appear. He pushed his chair back a little and looked around. He had picked a strategic position. He could see the entire room from this spot. It wasn't busy, there were only a few people in the place. Most were men, probably salesmen from the look of the sample cases. Most of the tables were vacant.

Mrs. Brassel was reasonably prompt. It was just a few minutes past ten when she entered the restaurant. She really was an exceptionally striking woman, with platinum blonde hair. She was dressed in a black astrakhan coat. Her appearance drew immediate attention from the few people in the restaurant. It was as if a sudden breeze rustled through the place.

Calmly she looked around the room. She spotted DeKok and approached him resolutely, with firm, long strides. There was a determined set to her mouth.

DeKok admired the feline suppleness of her body and the undeniable grace with which she moved. She is like a panther, he thought, with barely hidden claws.

Gazing at her, DeKok was convinced it was she who had telephoned Brets shortly before his death. Hers was the female voice with the German accent. Did she try to warn Brets? She knew something, but what?

Slowly he stood up.

"Good morning, Mrs. Brassel."

"Good morning, Inspector."

He helped her take her coat off and held her chair with old-world gallantry. A sweet scent of perfume rose from her hair.

"Coffee?"

"Please."

DeKok ordered from the approaching waiter. It was his third cup, but who was counting? Smiling, he sat down across from her. He looked intently at her, unashamed. She withstood his scrutiny with proud indifference.

"You're an extremely handsome woman," he said after a while. "Yes, indeed, extremely handsome." It sounded official, no more than the establishment of fact. He continued. "Trouble seems to be the lot of beautiful women. I sometimes wonder, is it beauty that attracts trouble or does trouble attract beauty?"

She smiled.

"I wouldn't worry about it."

The waiter arrived with the coffee.

Both were silent. DeKok stirred his coffee thoughtfully and stared at her right hand on the table. The hand shook a little.

"I take it," he said finally, in his most unconcerned tone of voice, "your husband sent you?"

"No! No," she repeated. "I came of my own accord. My husband knows nothing about this. He's in the office.

I found a babysitter for the children." She sighed deeply. "But I cannot stay long."

DeKok nodded, understanding.

"Well," he said with an inviting gesture, "you have the floor. I'm here to listen."

She nervously crushed an empty sugar wrapper. A nervous tic trembled at the corners of her full, sensuous lips.

"Well," urged DeKok, "you certainly didn't ask to meet me because of my irresistible charm."

She gave him a sweet smile. Her hand reached across the table. The tips of her fingers barely touched his arm. The touch, however slight, gave DeKok a warm feeling. His skin tingled.

"There is something reassuring about you," she said softly.

"I don't quite know," he answered sadly, "whether to be flattered or not. I'll take it as a compliment, although I can think of other things a man wishes to hear from a young, attractive female."

She looked at him with incomprehension.

DeKok pursed his lips and shook his head.

"Pay no attention to me," he said in a more serious tone. "My day started poorly and it isn't progressing in an upward direction. Please tell me what I can do for you."

"I'm worried."

"About your husband?"

She nodded.

"Yes. You see, he believes in precise analysis. Despite all the preparations and plans, I believe things can go wrong."

"Wrong how?"

She lowered her head and did not answer.

"What are you trying to say, Mrs. Brassel? What could go wrong with what?"

She gave him a bleak look.

"I'm sorry, Mr. DeKok. Please believe me. I wish I could be more specific. It would put my mind at ease. But I really cannot tell you."

DeKok narrowed his eyes.

"Then why did you ask to meet me?" He sounded annoyed. "Why did you come here? If you cannot be open with me, this meeting serves no useful purpose."

He rose as if to leave. She immediately placed a restraining hand on his sleeve.

"Please, sit down," she begged. "I want to ask you something. I have a request."

"A request?"

"Yes."

DeKok gestured expansively.

"Go on, then," he encouraged. "I can never deny the requests of beautiful women."

A wan smile flitted over her face.

"I," she sighed, "don't ask much."

"I'm listening."

She looked at him. Her eyes were beseeching.

"When you go home tonight, Mr. DeKok," she whispered, "you will find an invitation for a rummage sale in Oldwater, near where we live."

"Yes."

She moved a blonde strand away from her face.

"I urge you most earnestly to accept the invitation, Mr. DeKok. You and your wife should come to the sale."

DeKok shrugged his shoulders in a casual movement. "Why?"

She gave him a penetrating look.

"I already told you, my husband knows nothing about this. I do this on my own. I know the invitation has been sent. I also know why. My husband hopes you'll come. He is, however, of the opinion that your presence isn't strictly necessary. He expects enough people to attend the gathering, plenty who will recognize us. Perhaps he's right, but most people have bad memories for faces. Not you, Mr. DeKok, not you. You're a trained policeman, used to observing, used to remembering salient facts. That's why, you see, I want you to be there."

She spoke in a compelling voice, convincing, with barely controlled emotions.

"I have two small children, Mr. DeKok. It is unbearable thinking…"

"Pierre," completed DeKok, "could go to jail."

She nodded slowly, reluctantly.

"You understand."

DeKok picked up his cup and slowly drained the last of his coffee. Her words echoed in his head, resonating at a high frequency. After a while he replaced the empty cup and rubbed his chin in a pensive manner.

"You know the plans?"

"Yes."

"And you were the woman who called Brets at the Greenland Arms the night he was murdered?"

She nodded almost imperceptibly.

"Why?"

She did not answer.

DeKok pressed his lips together.

"Then I will tell you," he spoke bitterly. "You wanted to soothe your conscience with a telephone call. It was a miserable attempt. You called at eight o'clock. You *knew* it would be too late."

Her eyes threw sparks.

"I couldn't get through," she hissed.

"Otherwise you would have told Brets what was about to happen?"

She bent her head and remained silent. Her cheeks trembled, as if she was about to cry.

DeKok faced a dilemma. He did not know what to do next. He rubbed his lips with the back of his hand and looked at the woman across the table. How far dare he go?

"Mrs. Brassel," he said, hesitating about the words to choose, "I, eh, I could interrogate you officially right here, in the restaurant. It would be easy to mislead, make you admit things you would rather keep secret. Part of my training is in interrogation, so I know all the tricks. It would make my life so much easier if I could use your answers for my own purposes. You could lead me to other sources, or conclusions, which I could use against your husband."

He paused and rested his elbows on the table.

"I could do all that, but I will not."

He looked at her, his head cocked to one side.

"Please answer one question."

"Yes?"

"Who will be killed tonight?"

Mrs. Brassel paled. Her lips parted. She looked at him with wide, frightened eyes. She was stunned.

"Who," repeated DeKok, "will be killed tonight?"

A shrill, incoherent sound escaped her lips.

She recovered almost immediately. She stood abruptly, grabbed her coat, and bolted for the exit. She did not take the time to put her coat on. She fled, as if pursued by all the minions of hell.

DeKok watched her leave, unemotionally. He remained calm, seated, his broad face an expressionless mask.

The waiter approached.

"The lady was in a hurry," he concluded.

DeKok nodded and ordered his fourth cup of coffee.

17

Trouser legs rolled up to his knees, DeKok resembled an old fisherman from times gone by. He was at home, his painful feet in a tub of hot water with baking soda. He cursed. He cursed everything. He cursed his narrow shoes and the formal black suit he had worn to Jan Brets's funeral. He cursed Ma Brets, who had stained his shirt with mascara-laden tears. He cursed Cynthia Worden, attending the funeral dressed like a silly schoolgirl and behaving accordingly. Above all he cursed himself for staying so long in Utrecht, strolling aimlessly through unfamiliar streets. He'd wandered Utrecht until his painful feet had forced him to sit on a curb and untie his shoelaces.

In retrospect he understood that his only business in Utrecht had been to attend the funeral. There was nothing else to be accomplished there. Every time he ignored a warning from his feet, things went wrong. The solution to the riddle was not to be found in Utrecht. Jan Brets had lived there, that was all.

His wife approached with a fresh kettle of hot water.

"You want a little more hot water?"

DeKok lifted his dripping feet and looked at the stream of hot water with suspicion in his hawk's eyes.

"All right, hold off, though," he cried anxiously. "Not so much. I'm not a lobster!"

His wife laughed and felt the temperature of the water with concerned concentration.

"Just right like this."

DeKok carefully lowered his legs until his feet touched the water. Starting with the toes he slowly submerged his feet. After a painful grimace, a comfortable, idiotic smile appeared on his face.

DeKok's boxer looked patiently on from a corner of the room. Once the cursing stopped, the dog crept closer. DeKok petted the dog and gave his wife a friendly grin. Slowly the pain left his feet.

"Did you," he asked pleasantly, "receive an invitation this morning for some kind of rummage sale?"

She looked surprised.

"How did you know?"

DeKok laughed mysteriously.

"May I see it, please?"

She walked over to the small desk in the corner of the comfortable room and returned with the card.

"Here you are."

DeKok accepted the card from her and scrutinized it. It was a simple invitation to a rummage sale. The event was to be held in the building of the YMCA by the organization Oldwater Forward! There would be dancing after the sale. The proceeds were to benefit several Boy Scout groups in the little river town.

"This came by mail?"

His wife shook her head.

"It was delivered."

"How delivered?"

"A slender young man, about thirty." She pointed at a vase filled with tulips on a sideboard. "With flowers and a recipe."

DeKok grinned.

"Cake recipe?"

His wife sat down.

"Yes, you knew? A complicated recipe."

DeKok smiled at the questioning face of his wife.

"Try it sometime," he said, "success assured."

She looked at him searchingly.

"Jurriaan," she said in a compelling voice, "what does all this mean?"

DeKok's wife was the only one who sometimes called him by his first name. It was an unusual name, even in Holland. It came from one of the small islands in the Zuyder Zee. The island had long since become a part of the mainland as a result of the Dutch penchant for creating living spaces. In this case they had "simply" built a dike around large parts of the Zuyder Zee, pumped the water out, and built farms on what had once been the bottom of the sea. DeKok's island was now a rather large hill in the midst of a sea of corn. The harbor, where his father's fishing boat had been moored, was now a museum.

"Jurriaan," she repeated, "tell me about it."

"What?"

"Who was the young man? Why the flowers and the recipe? What about the invitation?"

DeKok raised both arms in the air.

"Not all at once, my dear. I don't have all the answers. Not yet. The good-looking young man must have been

Pierre Brassel. The recipe is from his very charming wife, and as for the invitation, we accept."

His wife did not take her eyes off him.

"Tonight," mocked DeKok, "we will mingle with the upper crust of Oldwater. We will admire and promote their attempts to create constructive leisure opportunities for Oldwater youth. We will cheerfully buy a few white elephants, try our luck at bingo, and trip the light fantastic until the early hours of the morning."

Mrs. DeKok listened more to the tone than to the content of his words. Something bothered her. Slowly she rose from her chair and stood behind him. With a gentle caress she placed her hand on his bristly gray hair.

"DeKok…"

"Yes?"

"Why are we accepting the invitation?"

DeKok wriggled his toes in the tub of soda water, creating tiny wavelets.

"Ach," he said, ducking the question, "a rummage sale, a dance…sounds like fun."

She smiled behind his back.

"Funny," she remarked, "I never knew you cared so much for village life."

DeKok sighed deeply.

"Now the serpent," he quoted, "was more subtle than any beast of the field."

She played her fingers through his hair.

"DeKok," her voice was insistent, "what's the reason for the invitation?"

He turned abruptly so that the water spilled from the tub.

"Murder," he said curtly.

The YMCA building was near the center of Oldwater. It was across from the bus stop in front of the town hall. It consisted of a miniscule lobby, a small auditorium, and a smaller stage. Off to one side of the building was a small gymnasium.

The place was pleasantly crowded.

Farmers came from the outlying areas around the village. Civil servants and businesspeople came from the bedroom community. Shopkeepers came from the small town. All had responded to the invitation. People walked around, looking at the offerings. A small musical combo was setting up on the tiny stage. Middle-aged ladies with permanent waves were everywhere, organizing, cajoling, and supervising. They were the driving force behind the organization Oldwater Forward! They sold tickets for door prizes, ran the bingo game, and took charge of the stalls. One could throw balls at a stack of tin cans or toss darts for prizes. One sharp-eyed old lady kept a close watch on the young girl in the kissing booth.

DeKok participated in everything except, in deference to his wife and the elderly chaperone, the kissing booth.

He threw balls and missed. He dunked his heavy body into a barrel filled with a lot of sawdust and a few meaningless prizes. He threw darts and missed. Last but not least, he had his fortune told by a gypsy fortune-teller, the wife of the local minister. She promised him a long life. "How long?" asked DeKok. The minister's wife smiled sweetly. "If you wish to live for more than a hundred years," she joked, "I must refer you to my husband." DeKok laughed heartily. Fine people, he thought, here in Oldwater. What a shindig to organize this late in the century. It took him back to his youth.

DeKok rarely forgot anything. He did not forget to keep his eyes open for Brassel. Brassel had not yet arrived. DeKok consulted his watch. It was a little after eight. He was surprised. According to his calculations, Brassel should have been present already. Unless, he reflected, he'd picked another time.

He nudged his wife.

"Do you see your young man anywhere?" he asked.

She stood on her toes and looked around.

"No, I don't see him. Is he supposed to be here?"

DeKok nodded.

"If I'm right, he's bound to show up. He needs us."

"For murder?"

DeKok grinned.

"You could say that."

He took his wife by the arm and together they pushed their way to the entrance.

"Are we leaving?"

"No, no, we're staying close. I want to know when he shows up."

They had almost reached the door when Brassel appeared.

DeKok withdrew slightly. He saw Brassel's eyes search the room. His wife followed him, holding six-year-old Ingrid by the hand. Mrs. Brassel, too, looked nervous. She pulled the child closer to her. It was an anxious moment.

DeKok pressed himself forward in the crowd. He observed Brassel catching sight of him. He forced his face into an expression of delighted surprise.

Brassel motioned to his wife. They approached, little Ingrid between them.

The usual formalities followed.

"I see," said Brassel, after everybody had met, "you accepted the invitation."

DeKok feigned a puzzled look. His wife intervened tactfully.

"This is the young man," she said cheerfully, "who delivered the invitation this morning."

"Oh," exclaimed DeKok, "so the invitation was *your* idea?"

Brassel laughed.

"Yes," he admitted. "Rather, it was my wife's idea. At first it was not part of my plan."

The two women quickly found they had common interests. Together they walked off in the direction of the bargain tables. DeKok had taken little Ingrid by the hand. He, Brassel, and the little girl followed the women.

The rummage sale was in full swing. There were sales of local embroidery, knitwear, and handicrafts of surprising, sometimes exquisite, quality.

"You were," DeKok said nonchalantly, "a few minutes late."

Brassel nodded.

"We hadn't planned to bring Ingrid," he explained, "but she woke just as we were ready to leave, coats on, walking out the door. When she saw we were going out, there was no way she was going to stay home without us. We had no other choice but to take her with us. First, though, we had to soothe her and get her dressed. It all took time."

DeKok laughed.

"Yes," he grinned, "the best-laid plans of mice and men."

Meanwhile he came closer to Brassel.

"Who," he whispered, "is to be killed tonight?"

Brassel looked shocked.

"I, eh, I d-don't understand you," he stuttered.

"Ach, come on, Brassel," DeKok's tone was full of reproach. "You understand me perfectly. It's silly to deny it. My wife and I and all the visitors here tonight have but one purpose. Why in the world would you need us to serve as an alibi unless there is another murder in the works?"

Brassel reacted strongly.

"What are you saying?" He hissed the question. "You have some nerve implying I'm only here because I need an alibi! Who says I need an alibi?"

DeKok grinned broadly.

"I do."

In passing he took a local beauty by the arm. The girl was selling carnations from a large wicker basket. She was a good-looking girl of about twenty years. She was healthy, with long blonde pigtails, soulful eyes, and a sweet mouth.

"What's your name?" asked DeKok.

"Francine," answered the girl.

"What else?"

"Francine Brakel."

DeKok smiled in a friendly way.

"Nice name." He pointed at Brassel.

"This gentleman wants to buy one of your carnations. But please pick a nice one. One that goes well with his handsome face."

He clicked his tongue.

"Have you noticed," he joked, "how handsome this gentleman is? A regular Apollo!" He grinned. "Oh, well," he continued, "perhaps not an Adonis, but in any case a man you will remember all your life. The sort of man you dream about."

The girl looked at Brassel's face and giggled. Still giggling she pinned a carnation to his lapel. Brassel just stood there, obviously embarrassed. He quickly pulled some money out of his pocket and paid. His face was sour.

From over the girl's shoulder, DeKok looked at him derisively. He enjoyed the moment. After the beauty and her basket had disappeared he said mockingly, "You see, Brassel, that's how you create an alibi. You don't need the police. I thought I'd give you a demonstration, because I don't feel much like being invited the next time you plan a murder."

He shook his head and spread his arms wide.

"But I do wonder how long you intend to keep it up. Really, seriously, Brassel, how many more murders are on the agenda?"

Brassel faced him fully. His eyes glowed angrily.

"What do you think I am?" His tone was indignant, offended. "I'm not an animal...not a *maniac*."

DeKok shrugged his shoulders in a manner meant to be irritating.

"How would I know? I've seen no psychiatric evaluation. What guarantees me you're not an antisocial deviant bent on destruction? Perhaps you have an irresistible urge to wipe out an entire community. At first glance, though, I'll admit you look quite normal."

DeKok's laconic manner, his calm, casual, conversational tone got under Brassel's skin. He was visibly upset. An excited blush spread over his face.

"I'm not crazy!"

He yelled so loud that people turned their heads and stared. Mrs. Brassel turned around. In that moment she correctly appraised her husband's loss of self-control. She stopped and came closer.

"What's the matter, Pierre?" she asked, concerned. "Who says you're crazy?"

Brassel did not answer.

She looked at DeKok. There was an icy, disapproving look in her eyes, not to say a hint of hatred.

DeKok grinned.

Just then little Ingrid, all but forgotten, suddenly cried, "*Hampelmann!*" The word exploded. It had the effect of a drumroll or a cannon shot. Nothing could have upset the Brassels more on this festive evening than the single word *Hampelmann* from the innocent mouth of little Ingrid.

The Brassels froze in their tracks.

DeKok watched with calm fascination. He registered what he saw, the shocked faces of the couple. Then, as if in slow motion, he felt Ingrid's hand being pulled from his own. He watched as Mrs. Brassel took the little girl into her arms in a protective gesture. He felt the nervous tension, but did not understand it.

Again the little girl repeated the word *Hampelmann* and pointed upward.

Somewhere in the maelstrom of his memories, DeKok searched for a handhold on this reality. He often prided himself on his inability to think in a straight line. He knew he was able to jump from one subject to another. He also knew he reached conclusions based on instinct and intuition as much as on logic. He had confidence and reason, backed by an enormous amount of experience. His eyes followed the little girl's outstretched finger.

In a single moment of revelation, he made a critical association. Myriad bits and pieces of information fell into place. All at once he understood the how and the why of the case. He stood before a simple stall featuring wooden marionettes with tall dunce caps. The dolls were hand-painted with little red noses. The artist had painted little yellow suns with minute rays on the cheeks. Each puppet wore a costume with black-and-white diamond shapes. Small strings hung down from the dolls. When the strings were pulled, the arms and legs would move in rhythmic unison. DeKok selected the best-looking harlequin.

He squatted down and motioned. Mrs. Brassel could not hold little Ingrid. The little girl struggled free and ran excitedly toward DeKok. Her eyes were bright with joy.

A friendly grin appeared on DeKok's face.

"*Hier mein Kind*," he said in his best German. "*Hier hast du deinen Hampelmann*."

18

Inspector DeKok rose slowly from his squatting position. The friendly, indulgent expression on his face disappeared as soon as Ingrid had her harlequin in her arms. His usually good-natured, craggy face was hard, almost grim.

He walked toward Brassel, his mouth compressed into a straight line, his heavy torso on a slight incline. His posture was so threatening that Brassel stepped back farther and farther.

DeKok walked on inexorably. He was an irresistible force of nature—nothing could stop him. Pierre Brassel fled, evading DeKok, until he could go no farther. He ran backward into a group of bantering farmers. Only when he tried to escape again did DeKok grab him. He placed his large, hairy hand on Brassel's chest and bunched the man's shirt into his fist.

"Who?"

Pierre Brassel panted heavily but did not answer. His nostrils quivered and there was fear in his eyes. Nervous tics ran along his cheeks.

"Who?"

Brassel remained silent.

DeKok tensed his arm and pulled him closer. Brassel's face was right in front of his own.

"WHO?" DeKok roared.

The raw bellow bounced against the walls. Several nearby visitors were shocked. All interest in charity abruptly disappeared. A crowd gathered around Brassel and DeKok. Neither bingo nor the fortune-telling minister's wife could compete with the sight of the two men. The hopeful expectation of a good fight held some onlookers spellbound.

Upset by the unexpected and unwanted commotion, a few of the elderly ladies rushed to the scene. With the tenacity of dowagers on the rampage, they tried to separate the two men. They were doomed to fail. DeKok did not let go.

"Who?" he roared again. "I will not stand by if I can still prevent it!" He shook the younger man so powerfully that he actually lifted him off his feet. His rage was monumental. "Damn you. You insect," he hissed. "Speak up!"

Brassel hung his head.

"Too late," he said softly. "It's too late."

DeKok released him. He took his wife by the arm and left the YMCA building, his head held high.

"I'll never go with you again...never again. If you no longer know how to behave, I won't be seen in public with you."

Mrs. DeKok was angry, shocked, and obstinate. Her bosom rose and fell with sheer indignation. Her face was red.

"The Brassels are such a nice couple. You attacked that poor man, like...like some hoodlum! How *dare* you? It's all because of the job. I know you're a policeman, but that's no reason to forget your manners. That was...it was *immoral!*"

DeKok gripped the steering wheel of his old car a little tighter and sighed.

"I am sorry, darling," he apologized. "You could not know how much I regret this." He was crestfallen. "You will come to understand. I had to try to save a life, no matter what it took. Only Pierre could have told me..." He paused. "He could have made it so much easier for everyone. Otherwise I would never have tried to force him. You believe me, don't you? You know how I loathe the use of force."

She looked at him from the side and studied the expression on his face.

"Sometimes I wonder," she said hesitantly. "It is hard to know what to think when you work your police tricks." She smiled suddenly. "Could we start with why we would receive or accept an invitation to a bazaar put on for and by people we do not know?"

DeKok shook his head.

"You don't have to understand," he smiled in response. "I'll explain it all to you later. For now, it's still a bit complicated and it would take too long."

She sighed.

"But it's about a murder, isn't it? That's what you said this afternoon."

"Yes, yes," he said, "it's about murder, all right, or rather about two murders."

"Two?"

DeKok nodded.

"Look," he explained patiently, "while we were enjoying the rummage sale with the Brassels, a second murder was being committed. What is more, both of them knew it. They knew it was going to happen."

"Where?"

DeKok shrugged his shoulders.

"I don't know."

"Who was being murdered?"

DeKok shook his head sadly.

"That I don't know either."

She laughed with just a tiny hint of contempt.

"What *do* you know?"

DeKok let the car slow down slightly and searched for a stick of chewing gum. His face was worried.

"Listen," he said in a hopeless tone of voice, "I know enough, believe me. I know enough to bring this case to a conclusion. As of today, Pierre Brassel understands I see through him. I had hoped to compel him to reveal the name of the second victim. But he did not. He kept his mouth tightly shut. I wonder why. It seems so senseless."

His wife scooted a little closer to him and placed a familiar hand on his knee. Her anger seemed to have dissipated.

"Perhaps," she said sweetly, "you don't know enough yet. It could be Pierre has some more surprises for you."

DeKok sighed.

"Perhaps. But now I know the why of the first murder. And although I don't know the name, I do know who was killed tonight."

Dumbfounded, DeKok's wife stared at him.

"But, b–but," she stammered, "if you knew that ahead of time, how could you let it happen?"

DeKok pressed his lips together.

"I let nobody be murdered," he said sharply. He was more abrupt than he had intended. "I didn't know until it was over. I only started to understand tonight. Call it stupidity, lack of insight." He shrugged his shoulders. "Whatever you call it, I did not see the solution in time. It's positively shameful that a six-year-old had to point the way, give me the clue."

"Clue?"

DeKok grinned, nodding his head.

"*Hampelmann.*"

DeKok lounged lazily behind his desk in the ancient, infamous police station. Reports on Jan Brets lay all over the desk. Before him were all the old documents, arrest reports, dispositions, depositions, and sentencing decrees he'd demanded. He had pored over them at home and had dragged them to the office. This time his reading went much more quickly than before. He knew exactly what he needed.

Next he went to see Celine, Dick Vledder's fiancée, to announce Vledder had to report to the office at once.

The attractive Celine protested vehemently, murmuring things about slave drivers. If looks could kill, the gray sleuth would have been reduced to burning embers. Vledder reluctantly stepped into the car.

"I just got here," growled Vledder. "I haven't seen her all week. So what's up? What's so all-fired important? You couldn't let me be for one night? I have a right to..."

DeKok waited patiently until the torrent of words had dried up. He understood his young partner, but he needed him.

"How can we find Renard Kamperman?"

"Who?"

"Renard Kamperman," repeated DeKok.

Vledder looked at him from the side, his mouth open.

"*Who is* Renard Kamperman?"

DeKok did not answer. He focused his concentration on guiding the car onto Warmoes Street. He did not like to drive. By his own admission he was the worst driver in the Netherlands, perhaps in all of Europe. He stopped in front of the station.

"Let us reason together," he said seriously.

They walked past the desk sergeant and climbed the stairs to the detective room. The file on Brets was still spread out on DeKok's desk.

Vledder pulled up a chair.

"All right. You have my attention," he said. "First tell me who Renard Kamperman is and what the good man has done to attract your attention all of a sudden."

DeKok rubbed his face.

"He died," he answered simply.

"Died?"

"Yes. A man named Renard Kamperman was murdered tonight. Don't ask me how I know. It would take too long to explain."

Vledder bit his lower lip.

"Do you know who did it?"

"Come again?"

"Who killed Kamperman?"

DeKok grinned.

"The same person who killed Jan Brets."

"What?"

DeKok nodded.

"Yes, the same killer."

"And that would be?"

Moodily, DeKok shrugged his shoulders.

"I don't know. I mean, I don't know yet! I have some suspicions, and I believe we have enough information to discover his identity."

Vledder nodded pensively.

"Do you know where this Kamperman was killed?"

DeKok shook his head, despair on his face.

"You're asking the same question my wife asked me an hour ago. It's a dumb question. Of course I don't know where he's been murdered. That is why I had to separate you from your Celine. You see, Dick, I knew Kamperman would be murdered before I knew his name. Brassel invited me to provide him a second alibi. While we were together, I discovered the motive for Jan Brets's murder." He sounded irritated with himself. "I know it sounds like the raving of a lunatic, but it's what happened."

Vledder sighed.

"Well, if I understand you correctly, Kamperman could have been killed anywhere. How do you propose we figure it out?"

DeKok scratched the back of his neck.

"There's only one thing to do. We have to look for Kamperman. Once we find his residence we'll have something to go on. I checked. The last known address is eight years old."

Vledder grimaced.

"Eight years? He's probably moved by now."

DeKok picked up the scattered pieces of the Brets file and threw them in a drawer.

"We don't have a choice," he said, a determined look on his face. "We have to check that address—it isn't much, but it's a start."

19

_____

"What can I do for you?"

The young woman looked shyly at the two men on the doorstep. She kept a hand on the doorknob.

DeKok turned his hat in his hands, visibly embarrassed.

"Renard Kamperman?"

She looked at him suspiciously.

"That's my husband, yes."

DeKok rubbed the back of his hand along his dry lips and sighed.

"We would like to talk with you for a moment. My name is DeKok, with, eh, a kay-oh-kay. This is my colleague Vledder. We're inspectors with the Amsterdam police."

The woman brought her hands to her throat in an automatic reflex.

"Has something happened?" she asked fearfully.

DeKok lowered his head somewhat.

"No," he answered, hesitating. "That's to say, we're not sure. Not exactly, I mean. It's all a bit difficult." He looked past her into the corridor. "Perhaps we could speak better inside? It's a bit windy out."

She nodded, slightly dazed.

"Come in."

She opened the door wider. Everything looked clean, fresh, and pleasant. The décor was modern, no frills. A tricycle in the corridor indicated a small child and a rack with drying diapers told of a baby.

"We did have a little trouble finding you," said DeKok pleasantly. "Happily one of your former neighbors remembered your husband. He said Mr. Kamperman had taken a job with a large firm in Gouda. That's all she knew, but it proved to be enough."

She offered the policemen a seat on a sofa.

"I don't know where my husband used to live." She sounded irked. "I have no desire to know. We've been married four years. Renard is a good father." She looked at DeKok as if he was an enemy. "To me, it's everything. Nothing else matters."

Apparently she wanted to blot out her husband's past. She was in denial, or suffering from selective memory. DeKok was certain, however, she was very well informed.

"Where's your husband?"

She did not answer.

"Where's your husband?" repeated DeKok, more insistent.

She looked at him as if trying to read his thoughts.

"Don't you know?" she asked dubiously, suspicion in her voice.

DeKok shook his head.

"No, Mrs. Kamperman," he said affably, "we do not know where he is, positively not. Please know we're not here to cause any problems. We're here as friends. As far as we know, your husband has done nothing illegal." He paused and sighed deeply. "Mrs. Kamperman," the tone of voice had changed, had a sad undertone, "we fear for your husband's safety. I believe your husband has been enticed to a specific place."

She blinked her eyes while she stared at him. Slowly she sank into an easy chair. She remained seated with her hands in her lap.

"Enticed?" she asked hoarsely.

DeKok nodded slowly.

"Yes," he said softly. "Enticed. I don't know how else to say it. I don't know how. Perhaps it was by letter. Perhaps someone approached him." He leaned toward her to better see her reaction. Then he asked, "Does the name Brassel mean anything to you?"

He saw the shock, and a wave of pity overcame him. She recognized Brassel's name. No doubt she had heard it. DeKok knew what it meant.

"Has Brassel been here, or did he write?"

She looked at him wildly.

"What's happened?" she cried, anxiety in her voice. "What do you want from me? What do you want with my husband? You said so yourself, he hasn't done a thing."

DeKok bit his lower lip.

"Mrs. Kamperman," he said soothingly, "please tell me, where was your husband supposed to be tonight at eight o'clock?"

She did not answer, but pressed her lips together defiantly. DeKok sighed, but his expression remained friendly, indulgent, understanding.

"My dear Mrs. Kamperman," he said earnestly, "please believe me. In your own best interest, tell me where I can find your husband."

She shook her head.

"No." Her voice was determined and stubborn. "I won't tell you anything. I promised not to talk about it."

DeKok swallowed.

"Mrs. Kamperman," he said. There was a dramatic, almost theatrical quality to his voice. "Upstairs are two children, *your* children. They're asleep. I do sincerely hope they keep their father, but I'm afraid it's already too late."

It was as if a sudden understanding came over her. DeKok's words had touched her. Her eyes widened, her chest rose and fell rapidly.

"What's going on?" she wailed. "What's happened to my Renard?"

DeKok rubbed his tired eyes with a weary hand.

"I really don't know," he admitted, bone tired. "However I suspect something serious may have happened."

He stood up and placed a comforting hand on the young woman's shoulder.

"Please try to cooperate with us. Tell us honestly where your husband went tonight. Perhaps we won't be too late."

She lowered her head.

"He went to Amsterdam."

"Where?"

"The Greenland Arms, a hotel."

"The Greenland Arms?"

"Yes, he was to meet somebody there."

Renard Kamperman was supine, with arms and legs stretched out wide. He had the same peculiar appearance of a wooden harlequin. The image of the harlequin was striking. The waxen face of Renard Kamperman was frozen in a grin. He grimaced, as had Jan Brets.

"Well, I'll be damned," exclaimed the concierge of the Greenland Arms. "Well, I mean, only the guy is different."

DeKok nodded.

"The guy is different," he repeated pensively, "only the victim has changed." He paused. "You should never swear, certainly not against yourself," he added gently.

He looked at Vledder, who was busy taking notes and measurements. DeKok had the sense of time standing still. He felt the world had stopped rotating on its axis, the sun had stopped rising and setting. It was surreal.

DeKok's expression was one of deep discouragement. Hands in his pockets, he looked around, searching for differences. He found none. Everything was exactly the same. Except for the victim.

He walked out of the room and counted the number of paces to the elevator. There were thirty paces, back and forth. When he was again in front of the door, he realized there should have been at least one more difference. He looked up. The number twenty-one was painted on the door.

Wildly, he took the concierge by an arm.

"Why," he cried furiously, "did you rent this room? Who had the unmitigated gall to break the seals?"

The concierge looked at him, astonishment on his face.

"But we were told we could."

"By whom?"

The concierge swallowed.

"Your...your own chief, your commissaris."

"*What*?"

"Yes, sir, our director called your commissaris several times to ask if the seals could be removed."

DeKok stared at him.

"Your director called personally?" His eyes narrowed.

The concierge nodded vehemently.

"Yes, yes. I was there myself. The director's calls, several of them, were all to the commissaris at Warmoes Street. The first time was shortly after you placed the seals. His request was denied. He cursed a blue streak."

"And?"

"During the following days he called regularly. Apparently he finally got permission yesterday afternoon...permission to break the seals, I mean. The word came right away, instructing us to remove the seals and ready the room for occupancy." He made a helpless gesture. "So, of course, we immediately obeyed the director's orders."

DeKok nodded.

"Yes, of course, I understand." He rubbed the bridge of his nose with his little finger. "I don't think," he began thoughtfully, "I met your director the last time, did I?"

The concierge shook his head.

"No, the director didn't come down until after you and your colleague had left. He lives upstairs, in the penthouse suite, you see. Since his illness, he doesn't concern himself with the actual running of the business as much. It's usually left in the hands of the department heads and the assistant manager. But somebody probably told him what happened."

"Who?"

"Not me."

"Who, then?"

The concierge shrugged his shoulders.

"I don't know. Could have been anybody, even a bellhop or a chambermaid."

DeKok sighed.

"How did he react? Was he upset about his hotel getting such notoriety?"

Slowly the concierge shook his head.

"He didn't say anything about it. After he found out he just asked me what had happened. I told him as much as I knew, also about the sealing of the room."

DeKok nodded slowly to himself.

"The list you gave me last time, I mean the list of personnel. Wasn't the name of the director on that list?"

The concierge grinned.

"No," he said indignantly, "he's the director, of course he wasn't on it."

DeKok hid his face in his hands and groaned.

20

Inspector DeKok continued to search around. Room twenty-one of the Greenland Arms looked normal once more. The nervous activity of the police had ceased and Renard Kamperman's corpse had been removed. Only a small bloodstain was still visible, the only remaining evidence of a crime.

"Are you finished?"

Vledder looked at the room one more time and nodded.

"I think so," he said with hesitation. "I don't think I missed anything." He took his notebook and read through his notes. "Yes," he concluded, "I've done everything I can."

DeKok nodded approvingly.

"Excellent, very good. Then you'd better go."

Vledder pointed at the door.

"What about the seals?"

DeKok shrugged his shoulders with a tired gesture.

"Ach, no." His voice was lethargic. "Leave it. It makes no difference, not anymore. We know everything. Anyway, there won't be any more murders, not here. This was the last vengeance of the harlequin."

Vledder looked at him with confusion.

"You seem convinced."

DeKok nodded, his face haggard.

"Yes, I am," he sighed. "Convinced and very sad." He gave Vledder a wan smile. "Come on, Dick, it'll be so late otherwise." He looked at his watch. "You can be in Gouda in no time. Be careful, don't speed. Please try to tell Mrs. Kamperman as gently as possible. She was already extremely upset. She needs to be told very gently. Try to comfort her as best you can. Locate relatives. By all means, she needs to know as soon as possible."

Vledder smiled uncomfortably.

"I'd much rather you came with me. You're so much better in these situations. I never know how to handle someone else's sorrow. I usually get so upset myself."

DeKok slapped him lightly on the shoulder in a fatherly, comforting way.

"That doesn't matter, Dick," he said. "Nothing against that. Sorrow is universal."

Vledder sighed.

"You're really not coming along?"

DeKok shook his head.

"I'm staying here."

"In the hotel?"

"For the time being. I promised myself an interview with the hotel director."

Vledder nodded.

"Well, all right, then," he said, a melancholy look on his face. "I'm off then. I can just picture what'll be waiting for me in Gouda, a crying woman and terrified kids. I hope she has family nearby, otherwise I may have to wake the neighbors."

DeKok nodded.

"Do the best you can," he said simply.

A gruff expression on his face, his old felt hat far back on his head, DeKok stood in front of the concierge's desk. He rapped on the wood with a flat hand.

Startled, the concierge looked up.

"Oh," he stammered, confused, "I didn't know you were still on the premises. I thought you'd left at the same time as your colleague."

DeKok grinned maliciously.

"No, my friend," he said threateningly, "I'm still here. I stayed behind, stayed to have a nice little chat with your director."

"Oh."

"Yes," answered DeKok. "Now will you be so kind as to announce me?"

The concierge sighed deeply.

"Mr. Gosler," he hesitated, "is ill. Very ill, I must say. For months now, he hasn't received anyone in his suite. This is most certainly not a good time. It's well past midnight."

DeKok forced his lips into a broad smile.

"I know what time it is, my friend," he remarked with syrupy sarcasm, "you don't have to tell me." He shook his gray head. "I didn't ask you the time, now did I? No, I just asked you to announce me to your director. That's all."

The concierge pulled his head between his shoulders.

"I'm afraid," he said, avoiding the issue, "I…"

That is as far as he progressed.

DeKok leaned over the desk. In a casual, irresistible manner, he grabbed the man by the neck. He pulled him from behind his desk.

"Come, friend," he hissed, "show me the way."

The concierge struggled in DeKok's grip.

"If you'll permit me," he squeaked, "I'll call ahead. That would be better, I think."

DeKok released him.

"Excellent, a good idea. Call him first. But be sure to let him know that I *insist* on speaking with him."

DeKok raised a cautioning finger.

"And, just in case mister director has some exalted but mistaken idea of his own importance, you will enlighten him. It would be a serious error were either of you to keep me out here, cooling my heels. Regardless of any law to the contrary, I will personally break down his door."

The concierge studied DeKok's determined face and swallowed nervously.

"Really," he exclaimed, impressed and scared, "I really believe you'd do it."

DeKok grimaced.

"You can bet your life."

"I shall seriously complain about you. You can depend on that. The commissaris at Warmoes Street is a personal friend of mine. He wouldn't approve of you bothering a seriously ill person in the middle of the night. You're acting outside the law. You overstep your authority, yes, you're far exceeding your authority."

DeKok nodded toward the man seated across from him. He gave him a pitying smile. The director's stern look melted into weariness. He'd tried his best to be as menacing as his speech. His behavior was a sad demonstration of physical deterioration. He rested his head against the high back of the chair and wheezed.

DeKok looked at him, outwardly unmoved. The inspector searched the face intently, looking for a family resemblance. The genes were undeniably there. The man had blonde hair and blue eyes. Long, thin hands deformed by arthritis emerged from the sleeves of an oversized robe. DeKok judged the man to be about fifty years of age, but realized immediately it was a hunch. The face was wan, marked by a stealthy disease that had left indelible signs of its progress. Fredrich Gosler looked at least fifteen years older than his true age.

"It's strange," sighed DeKok, "singular, really. Everybody connected to this case knows exactly how to tell me the limits of my authority. The same people keep saying a great deal about justice." He shook his head in displeasure. "You see, the latter bothers me to no end. We know from history that peace is the main topic of conversation just before a war."

Gosler leaned forward.

"I don't understand you," he said softly.

DeKok grinned his irresistible grin.

"I do believe your intelligent brother-in-law would have understood me, Mr. Gosler. What I mean is most wars are waged in the name of peace. A great deal of *injustice* is practiced in the name of justice."

For a long time Gosler looked at him thoughtfully.

"You," he faltered, "you know why those two had to die?"

DeKok did not answer at once. He rubbed the corners of his eyes with thumb and index finger. It was a tired gesture. A sudden lethargy overcame him. It was as if the tension under which he had worked for the last few days had suddenly snapped as the adrenalin flow had stopped. He could not take pleasure in reaching his goal. On the contrary, it made him feel extremely depressed.

"Yes," he answered after a long pause. "I know why you orchestrated the murders."

"And?"

"What?"

"Well, what do you think of the motive?"

DeKok swallowed.

"I'm sorry," he said, shaking his head, "no matter how you slice it, I cannot admire you."

Gosler's face fell. His fingers cramped around the armrests of the chair. The knuckles showed up white. Slowly he pushed himself into a standing position.

With his arms tightly pressed against his body, almost as if he were on parade, he stood in front of DeKok.

"Then, Inspector," he spoke formally, "you must arrest me at once."

DeKok looked up. He gazed at the scarecrow figure. Gosler's robe hung around him in large folds. His dull eyes sank into their sockets, his prominent cheekbones added to the appearance of a death mask. DeKok shook his head.

"No," he answered slowly, "I don't think I will."

Gosler looked at him with surprise.

"But you *must* arrest me!" he cried out. "I insist. It's your duty."

DeKok shrugged his shoulders in a careless gesture.

"Ach, Mr. Gosler," he said moodily, "please sit down. You're much too ill to stand for long. In addition, you cannot order me to do anything. As far as my duty is concerned, *I* will determine what that is."

The hotel director hesitated an instant longer. Then he lowered himself shakily back into his chair. His sallow complexion turned gray. DeKok realized how much effort it must have taken the man to handle the heavy hockey stick with such deadly force. Gosler seemed to read his mind.

"I'm losing ground rapidly, especially these last few days." He sounded hopeless. "I'm glad I was able to complete my task. I was afraid I would not be able to do so."

He paused and sighed.

"I must insist you place me into custody, so the world will know what I have done and why."

DeKok looked at him sharply.

"No, Mr. Gosler," he said, shaking his head. "It is knowledge the world must never know. If your story becomes common knowledge, too many people may rationalize your actions. Perhaps there will be a few in similar circumstances. That is, people unable to be touched by human justice due to illness or impending death."

An ugly grin appeared on Gosler's small mouth.

"If you don't arrest me, I call the commissaris. If he doesn't respond, there's always the press."

DeKok nodded morosely.

"I take it," he said, "that my commissaris is not yet informed?"

"Not yet."

DeKok stared a long time at nothing at all. There was a resigned, sphinxlike look on his face. After a few minutes he stood up. He took the ivory-colored phone from a side table and placed it in the lap of the astonished Gosler. Then he sat down again and gave the sick man a friendly, challenging nod.

"You know the number of my chief?"

Confused, Gosler nodded.

"Excellent," said DeKok, "then you may call him now."

Gosler looked at him suspiciously.

"*Now?*"

DeKok gestured.

"But of course. Why not? As you are talking to the commissaris and/or informing the press, I will be headed directly to Oldwater. There I will take your sister and your brother-in-law into custody. Please note, *regardless* of the children."

He paused.

"And please, Mr. Gosler," he continued, "do not think for one single moment they will get off scot-free. Laws, rules, and norms will only guarantee a free society as long as everybody lives accordingly. You see, Mr. Gosler, if necessary, I will perjure myself. If once is not enough, I will perjure myself again and again. Please disabuse yourself of any ideas about my trustworthiness, my honesty. If I have to, I can be just like you—a man without any scruples."

Gosler's eyes narrowed.

"Is that a threat?"

"You can take it any way you want. Just be certain of one thing: if you confess as the perpetrator or make public your deeds in any way, your sister and your brother-in-law will go to jail as accessories before, during, and after the fact."

Gosler studied his face for a long time, gauging the seriousness of the threat.

"Yes," he concluded finally, "you would."

Grinning, DeKok picked up the telephone from Gosler's lap and replaced it out of reach.

"Come," he said in a friendly tone of voice, "let us speak about justice."

Gosler gave him a tired nod.

21

Furious, the commissaris clawed for the phone. The report regarding the most recent murder was in front of him. It was an extremely short report, no more than half a page. It contained the information that the corpse of a man had been found in room twenty-one of the Greenland Arms. The man was identified as Renard Kamperman, age twenty-six, and the circumstances at the crime scene showed a marked similarity to those of the Jan Johannes Brets murder. That was the sum total of the content. That was all. The commissaris was extremely displeased. He banged his fist on the desk and yelled loudly into the telephone.

"Have DeKok report to me!"

Inspector Corstant, who happened to pick up the telephone in the detective room, calmly remarked he could not understand the speaker.

"Have DeKok report to me," repeated the commissaris, calmer.

"I'm sorry," replied Corstant.

"What?"

"DeKok isn't here."

"What about Vledder?"

"He's here."

"Good, have Vledder report."

"As you wish," replied Corstant quietly. He replaced the receiver and looked around. When he spotted Vledder he motioned him closer.

"The boss wants you, Dick. Better take a deep breath, he's really upset."

Vledder shrugged his shoulders.

"It's not my fault," Vledder smirked. "I've always been very nice to him." He put his coat on, arranged his tie, and left to meet his commissaris.

The commissaris was beside himself. He paced up and down his office like a caged lion and vented his torrent of anger and frustration on poor Vledder.

"Two murders in three days," he roared, "and what does it get me?" He banged the desk with his fist every time he passed by it. "What do I have to show for it? Eh? Answer me that! I'll tell you what I have. Two microscopic reports, *that's* what I have! And what's in those reports? I'll tell you what's in those reports. Nothing! Absolutely nothing!" He raised both arms despairingly toward the ceiling. "What have you two accomplished while you've been too busy to report? Am I perhaps privileged to know? So, tell me, Mr. Inspector, who's the boss around here? *DeKok or me?*"

Vledder dared a cautious remark.

"You are, Commissaris."

"Right," he hollered, "I am! *I* know that and *you* know that! But does DeKok know that? Perhaps you could ask him!"

Vledder swallowed.

"I will, sir," answered Vledder earnestly.

The commissaris controlled himself and sat down behind his desk. Venting his rage had soothed his nerves. He was visibly relieved. He stroked his gray hair with a steady hand and indicated to Vledder to sit down.

"Three murders in two days," he lamented.

"Two murders in three days," corrected Vledder.

The commissaris gestured impatiently.

"Yes, well, that's what I mean. This is just the kind of thing the press eats up—both murders in the same hotel, actually in the same room. There has to be a connection. It's too much of a coincidence. You were there, weren't you, I mean after the deaths of Brets *and* Kamperman?"

Vledder nodded.

"Both times," he admitted.

"And, eh, what does DeKok say about it?"

"DeKok is never very forthcoming in a situation like this. The last time we spoke he gave me the impression he was close to a solution. He did mention he had sufficient evidence to catch the killer."

The commissaris nodded thoughtfully.

"So, is that what he said?"

"Yes, sir. You should know DeKok isn't a braggart. If DeKok says—"

The commissaris did not want to hear any more praise. He stood up. He looked down on Vledder with a penetrating look from beneath his bushy eyebrows.

"Have DeKok report to me."

It was an order.

Vledder made an apologetic gesture.

"I really don't know where he is. I called his home this morning, but he isn't there. I spoke to his wife. She doesn't know where he is either."

The commissarial face was getting dangerously red. He stretched his arm in the direction of the door.

"Then you find him. For all I care you put out an APB on him, but find him!"

It echoed through the room.

Vledder nodded.

"Yes, sir," he said timidly. "Yes, sir, I will."

Then he fled from the room.

DeKok guided his personal VW through the old inner city of Amsterdam. He had just completed an extended visit to Dr. Brouchec. Now he was hunting for a parking spot as close as possible to the respected firm of Brassel & Son.

The interview with the doctor had confirmed his opinion about Fredrich Gosler's illness. Gosler, himself, had no illusions.

At first the good doctor had been reluctant to cooperate. But when DeKok threatened to arrest Fredrich Gosler and went on to describe the lurid conditions in the cells at Warmoes Street, the doctor had relented. In the strictest confidence, so he told DeKok, he had shared his medical opinion and prognosis. DeKok had asked for a written statement, but the doctor had categorically refused.

"Just wait," he had said.

But it was exactly the waiting that put DeKok in a predicament.

When he finally found a place for his car, he got out and ambled over to the Brassel office. His face was serious. The creases in his forehead were deeper and sharper than usual. He had a plan, but he knew the risks involved. He also knew the letter and spirit of his official instructions. He had a booklet, with several supplements, containing specific official responses to any given situation. DeKok had no special love for rules and regulations. People were important to him. His greatest challenge was weighing the needs of people against the requirement to strictly adhere to "the book."

He climbed the bluestone steps to the front door and rang the old-fashioned brass bellpull. After a minute the heavy black-lacquered door opened. A green-eyed girl confronted him. There was a dimple in her left cheek. DeKok lifted his hat with a flourish and smiled.

"My name is DeKok," he said amiably, "DeKok with, eh, a kay-oh-kay. Please tell Mr. Brassel I want to speak to him."

A bit shyly, Vledder adjusted his tie.

"Mrs. DeKok," he said beseechingly, "do you really not know where your husband is? The commissaris is furious. He's yelling and screaming for DeKok, justifiably so. I mean, Mrs. DeKok, you know how I like your husband, but he hasn't been in the office for more than three days. That's absurd, let's face it."

Mrs. DeKok nodded.

"You're right, Dick, it is absurd. I can't understand myself what's come over him." She laughed at him.

"Of course I know where he is. But he told me that he wasn't available to anyone."

Vledder pulled a hurt face.

"Not even to me?"

She smiled tenderly.

"Come back at eight tonight, Dick. I'll make sure he's here."

22

DeKok greeted his young colleague heartily. He shook his hand for a long time, placed a friendly arm around his shoulder, and led him to the cozy living room. DeKok's face beamed. He seemed genuinely please about Vledder's visit.

"I do believe, Dick," he said jovially, "I owe you an explanation. Of course, I would have told you everything in time, but my wife took pity on you. She persuaded me to explain everything now."

Mrs. DeKok winked at Vledder.

"Really," she said with a smile, "it wasn't all that hard."

"But my wife is right," added DeKok seriously, "why not, after all? We've been working together for some time. I know I can trust you." He gestured. "And I need that trust. You see, I must ask you to keep this secret. You can't talk about anything I tell you, for the time being. Please do not reveal anything to the commissaris—especially not the commissaris. You must understand that I'm not avoiding him for no reason."

Vledder looked surprised.

"Is he involved?"

DeKok laughed.

"No, not really, thank goodness. But if he knew the whole story, he might force me to arrest the murderer. And I don't want to."

Vledder looked at him with disbelief.

"You don't want to?"

DeKok shook his head.

"No, I do not. I've a number of reasons for that, reasons I'll try to explain in the course of the evening."

He pointed at some comfortable leather armchairs.

"Come on, Dick, pull up a pew."

He walked over to a cabinet, returning with a bottle of French cognac. He showed the label.

"What do you think?"

Vledder nodded wholehearted approval of the choice.

DeKok took a couple of large snifters and warmed them gently over a small flame. Then he poured with total concentration. A connoisseur, DeKok loved good cognac. He savored the stimulating aroma, the tantalizing taste, the warming glow. A good glass of cognac was a sensuous pleasure to DeKok, total bliss.

"I have," he started after his first sip, "made a lot of mistakes in this case. Mistakes are almost inevitable in our profession. During every investigation, especially at the start, we grope. Every step, no matter how carefully taken, can lead in the wrong direction. We can never be afraid to make mistakes. People who are afraid to make mistakes avoid making decisions. It begins with circumventing and ends in fearful inaction, something peace officers cannot afford. No, Dick, I've never been afraid to make mistakes, never dodged decisions."

He took another sip and replaced his glass carefully.

"But, to business," he continued. "From the first it was certain Pierre Brassel couldn't possibly be the perpetrator. He produced incontrovertible alibis for both murders, making him untouchable. As you know, it was clear he was in contact with the killer. He told us he was completely aware of his plans and cooperated with those plans. He was a sympathizer, but who was the real murderer? Who was the man behind Brassel? Intriguing questions, to say the least. What came to occupy me was the *why*. As Jan Brets was dying, Brassel was playing a dangerous game, revealing outright complicity! So the motive became the key."

He glanced at Vledder, moved himself more comfortably in his chair. His hand strayed to the glass beside him, but he controlled the movement.

DeKok continued, "The usual motives didn't seem to apply. As you said aptly, they didn't compute. We found no connection between Brets and Brassel, at least not a connection that would imply a motive. Brets's murder seemed senseless. But Brets was not an *incidental* victim, on the contrary. Brets was carefully selected as the victim. Brassel sought him out and enticed him to take a room at the Greenland Arms."

DeKok raised an index finger in the air.

"What determined the choice of victim? I mean, why Brets? After all, he was a relatively unsuccessful burglar from Utrecht, a minor thug, right? Who would benefit from his death? We knew early on there was no direct connection between Brets and Brassel. I concluded there had to be an indirect connection, an indirect motive. The only way to unravel this was through the man behind Brassel, the real killer. But who was that?" DeKok grinned. "I kept thinking like that, in circles, always the same questions."

"I haven't heard any mistakes yet," observed Vledder.

DeKok sighed.

"We'll get there. As you will remember, we visited Brassel in Oldwater the day after the murder of Brets. We met Brassel's wife. Because of certain remarks, but more so because of her behavior, I left with the distinct impression the real murderer could be found within the Brassel family circle. It was a good hunch, it certainly provided a reasonable explanation for Pierre's behavior. After all, we make sacrifices for family. It seemed to me Pierre might, indeed, play his little games to help a family member."

DeKok made a grand gesture.

"If I had continued that train of thought at the time, I might have been able to prevent the murder of Renard Kamperman."

Vledder, his drink forgotten, looked at his mentor with astonishment.

"But why didn't you?"

DeKok gave Vledder a weary smile.

"Simply because I overestimated Brassel's intellect and his knowledge of the law."

"I don't follow you."

DeKok grinned ruefully.

"Do you remember we discussed the so-called warning note after we found Brets? Brassel became visibly upset when I lied to him. When I told him we hadn't found the note under the corpse. From his reaction I concluded that Brassel placed an inordinate amount of importance on this warning note. I was right!"

DeKok sighed deeply.

"At that time, though, I came to the wrong conclusion. Had the killer been a family member, Brassel would not have had to warn the victim. He *did* warn Brets, though. Therefore I concluded the real perpetrator was not a member of his family."

Mrs. DeKok leaned toward her husband.

"You mean," she said slowly, "that Brassel wouldn't have had to write a warning note if the killer were a member of his own family?"

DeKok nodded.

"That's right. He didn't have to inform the police, nor the intended victim. Since it concerned his own family, he could have invoked the right of extenuation."

"Right of extenuation?"

"Yes, that's what we call it here. According to Dutch law, nobody has to cooperate in the criminal prosecution of a blood relative. Most countries have something similar. The best-known example is the Fifth Amendment to the Constitution of the United States. It prohibits self-incrimination. In other words, it says no one has to testify against himself or herself. The laws in most countries also prevent a husband from testifying against his wife, and vice versa. Dutch law goes further. In Holland, so-called Fifth Amendment rights extend to self and first-degree relatives: wives, sons, daughters, parents, siblings. Anyway, Brassel did not know that, or he did not understand it. It doesn't matter, I was misled, regardless."

Vledder looked at him searchingly.

"Misled?" he asked.

DeKok rubbed his face with both hands.

"Yes," he sighed, "the murderer *was* a member of his immediate family."

Mrs. DeKok rose from her chair.

"How about some coffee?" she proposed.

DeKok nodded agreement, glancing at the bottle of cognac with regret. He lifted his glass and drained it. Then he poured himself another measure and raised his eyebrows at Vledder. Vledder hastily agreed a refill would be most welcome.

Mrs. DeKok watched with an indulgent smile.

"Well, what about coffee?" she repeated.

"Yes, darling," said DeKok, "and some of that cake, you know, from Mrs. Brassel's recipe."

Mrs. DeKok looked at him with mocking eyes.

"Why don't you call it harlequin cake?"

DeKok laughed briefly.

"Yes." He smiled at his wife. "Why not? Coffee and harlequin cake."

Vledder could hardly contain his patience. He could have done without the intermezzo. He would much rather listen to DeKok unravel the rest of the story. But he knew his partner. The gray sleuth was not to be hurried.

In due course, Mrs. DeKok returned with coffee and cake. Meanwhile she chatted cheerfully about Mrs. Brassel's marvelous recipe. The atmosphere was relaxed, as though solving murders was the furthest thing from their minds. Finally Vledder could stand it no longer. He edged closer to the front of his chair.

"How," he asked with barely contained impatience, "did you discover the killer was a member of the family?"

"*Hampelmann.*"

Vledder did not understand the cryptic remark.

"*Hampelmann?*"

DeKok nodded.

"Yes. It's the German word for harlequin."

"It doesn't mean a thing to me," replied Vledder, annoyed. "I only know both Brets and Kamperman were found in positions reminiscent of marionettes...harlequins. What does the German word have to do with it?"

DeKok sighed.

"*Hampelmann* is very much to the point. The corpses were purposely arranged in that position."

"Got it, but why?"

DeKok smiled faintly.

"As a symbol."

"Symbol? A symbol of what?"

"Justice."

"Justice?"

"Yes, Dick, justice. To understand, we have to go back in time a little."

He drained his cup and Mrs. DeKok almost immediately refilled it.

"A few years before World War II, a certain Heinrich Gosler was arrested by the Nazis. Gosler's wife, a Jewish girl, fled to Holland, taking her two small children with her. She got to Haarlem. She had a brother living in Haarlem. Jacob Hampelmann, the brother, had fled Germany years earlier. He owned an antique business there. At considerable risk to herself, Frau Gosler returned to Germany after about a month. Her purpose was to somehow rescue her husband. It is likely the Nazis soon caught her. Nothing further was ever heard of the Goslers, husband or wife. As far as anyone knows, they perished in a concentration camp."

He paused briefly, reflected.

"The two children, Fredrich and Liselotte," he resumed, "stayed in Haarlem with their Uncle Hampelmann. The antique dealer took care of them as if they were his own. He provided each of the children an excellent education. How he managed to do that under the circumstances, under the noses of the German occupation forces, would make a heroic saga, no doubt. He managed, one way or the other. Naturally the children were devoted to their Uncle Hampelmann."

Thoughtfully, he rubbed the bridge of his nose with a little finger. Vledder and Mrs. DeKok hung on his every word.

"On to our victims. About eight years ago, Jan Brets and Renard Kamperman met in one of our incomparable reform institutions. A juvenile judge had placed both boys, seventeen and eighteen, respectively, in reform school. Jan Brets had endangered life and property in and around Utrecht. Young Kamperman had committed a series of burglaries in and around Haarlem. He had also failed in an attempt to burglarize Hampelmann's antique shop. Brets and Kamperman exchanged experiences and ideas. Kamperman told Brets about Hampelmann, who was generally known to be a very rich man. According to Kamperman, he'd failed to rob Hampelmann because the old antique dealer was 'as alert as a stinking German shepherd.' Brets had a remedy, which he shared."

He sighed deeply. Then he continued.

"Oh, yes, Brets knew how to fix it. If he got his hands on Hampelmann, the old man would sleep, never to wake. This pair planned cold-blooded murder and burglary in reform school. The very next weekend they earned passes for good behavior. The first night out they hitched a ride to Haarlem, bought a hammer, and bashed in old Hampelmann's head. The total proceeds of the robbery amounted to less than ten euros."

Mrs. DeKok shook her head in horrified astonishment.

"But that's terrible," she exclaimed.

"Indeed, terrible. Fredrich and Liselotte were extremely upset, to say the least. They were devastated. Neither was at home when it happened. Fredrich worked in a hotel, where he was groomed for management. Liselotte was staying with Pierre Brassel, her fiancé. Brets and Kamperman were soon apprehended. Both confessed. The crime scene investigation revealed how strenuously the elderly gentleman defended himself against his attackers. Brets had hit him so many times with the hammer he could not have been saved, death was inevitable. Fredrich Gosler wasn't spared any details. He went into a savage rage and he swore that he would avenge his uncle's murder."

"The seed for more murders," interrupted Vledder.

"Exactly," agreed DeKok, "the seed had been planted for more murders."

They remained silent. Fredrich Gosler's vengeful hatred had taken possession of them, as if the murders were being contemplated anew.

Mrs. DeKok moved uneasily in her chair.

"You know," she said earnestly, "I can understand how Fredrich Gosler would come to think that way. Had he laid hands on those two guys right after his uncle's murder, people would have understood. He'd have been guilty of acting on overpowering emotion. Not that he would have been justified in killing those two, mind you. By now, though, eight years have passed…"

DeKok bit his lower lip thoughtfully.

"You're right. Gosler's emotions after the vicious murder of his uncle might well have overwhelmed him. But Brets and Kamperman went to jail. Gosler's rage had plenty of time to cool. Gosler kept an eye on both men. He learned that neither man had served a full sentence. We have our much-touted system of rehabilitation and parole, you know. Imagine Gosler's chagrin when his uncle's murderers walked. Needless to say, Fredrich Gosler was outraged. He discussed this miscarriage of justice with his sister and brother-in-law, Pierre Brassel. All three agreed no justice had been done on behalf of Uncle Hampelmann. Fredrich proposed the idea of belated executions."

Vledder looked up.

"That sounds familiar."

DeKok nodded.

"Yes, I guess it would. Pierre Brassel made a mistake, right at the beginning. During our first meeting at the station, Brassel wondered aloud why he would take risks for a murder like that of Jan Brets. He said, 'It would be too silly to risk all that for a somewhat belated murder.' You remember? He swallowed the last word, but the word was meant to be *execution*."

Mrs. DeKok made a vague gesture.

"So, they accepted Gosler's idea at once?" she asked.

"No, Pierre Brassel was against it. He didn't want to go through with it. He was really an outsider, after all. He thought a lot more soberly about vengeance than his wife and her brother. He thought it was insane to risk their lives, family, and position executing the likes of Brets and Kamperman. Brassel is a snob. To him they were inferior beings, unworthy of the attention of a gentleman."

"Wha-what changed?" Vledder stammered. "I don't understand. The killings took place after all."

"Yes, but for a different reason," said DeKok.

"A different reason?"

"Cancer."

He remained silent. In his mind's eye he saw the sick man. The flat eyes, the hollow cheeks, the half-paralyzed mouth that spoke of justice.

"Yes," he continued, "Fredrich Gosler became ill with cancer. A forthright doctor told him that he had maybe six months left."

DeKok rubbed his eyes with a thumb and an index finger.

"The rest is easily deciphered. Gosler's wish in the last six months of his life was to avenge his uncle, to see justice done. He asked his brother-in-law, Pierre Brassel, to help."

Mrs. DeKok gave him a compassionate look.

"And," she asked, "this time Brassel was willing to cooperate?"

"Brassel was in a difficult position. In principle he agreed with his wife's brother. There had been no justice for Uncle Hampelmann. But he was still not inclined to take unnecessary risks for futile vengeance. Also, by nature, he was a lot more humane. Brassel believed the criminals could be rehabilitated, maybe *had* been rehabilitated. He didn't think Jan Brets was still the murderous maniac who had split Hampelmann's head with a hammer. He pleaded for a test."

"A test?" asked Vledder.

"Indeed, a test. He wanted Jan Brets to be placed in a hypothetical situation in which he would have the same choice."

"The same choice?"

"Yes," answered DeKok patiently. "He would give Brets a choice to kill...or not to kill."

"Ah, I get it. He chose to murder the old watchman."

"Exactly. Brassel approached Brets with a lot of garbage about a gang, an organization." He raised his index finger in the air. "He alluded to a rich haul at Bunsum & Company. He suggested the old night watchman would have to be eliminated. He even supplied Brets a weapon, a lead-reinforced hockey stick. It was clear that anybody who was hit on the head with *that* instrument would not survive the experience. But Brets cheerfully accepted the stick and the assignment. He declared no qualms about taking care of the old man."

"Thereby signing his own death warrant."

"Yes. Brets failed the test."

Mrs. DeKok was visibly upset. She shook her head, as if to clear it. Imagine setting up a cold-blooded test to determine if someone would live or die a violent death. It was more than she could bear.

"What about Kamperman?" she cried.

"Pierre Brassel hadn't the luxury of delaying matters," he answered gravely. "Perhaps he could have delayed the second murder, which certainly put him at further risk. Gosler, however, was facing down his own death. Brassel had argued at length to get Gosler to agree to the first test. Jan Brets proved to be as ready to commit murder as he had been in the past."

DeKok shook his head in despair.

"When Brassel asked for a test for Kamperman," he continued, "Gosler wouldn't hear of it. Time was pressing, you see. Fredrich Gosler was getting weaker by the day. The disease progressed faster than the doctor had estimated. If he was to complete his self-imposed task, they had to proceed."

"So Renard Kamperman didn't have a chance?" Vledder questioned. It sounded bitter.

"That's the most tragic part of the whole situation. Kamperman *had* been rehabilitated. He had turned over a new leaf, moved from his old surroundings and married. He and his wife had two small children and he had become a respectable father, husband, and wage earner."

DeKok stopped talking. His final words still hung in the room.

After a long silence, Mrs. DeKok spoke.

"*Justice* can be a terrible word," she said.

DeKok pushed his lower lip forward and nodded.

"Sometimes," he agreed somberly.

Vledder was still deep in thought.

"Why," he asked after a while, "don't you finish this case in the normal, prescribed manner?"

"What do you mean?"

"Well, why not arrest Gosler?"

"No, I won't do that. Please understand it is not because of Gosler, or because of his illness. Certainly not because I sympathize with his motives, but because I'm afraid."

"You? Afraid?"

"Yes, I'm afraid of the consequences. Cancer is not exactly a rare disease. Suppose people in the end stages of disease get the idea it is acceptable to take justice into their own hands. So they get into the private execution business. The consequences don't bear thinking about. That's why it's better for the Case of the Dead Harlequins never to become public knowledge."

It was already late at night when Vledder went home.

"Say hello to the office for me tomorrow," said DeKok in parting.

Vledder smiled.

"When are you coming back?"

"As soon as Fredrich Gosler has passed on. According to the doctor, it's only a matter of days. Not until then will I report to the commissaris."

He made a simple gesture, shrugged his shoulders.

"You cannot arrest the dead."

ABOUT THE AUTHOR

A. C. Baantjer is one of the most widely read authors in the Netherlands. A former detective inspector of the Amsterdam police, his fictional characters reflect the depth and personality of individuals encountered during his nearly forty-year career in law enforcement.

Baantjer was honored with the first-ever Master Prize of the Society of Dutch-Language Crime Writers. He has also been knighted by the Dutch monarchy for his lifetime achievements.

The sixty crime novels featuring Inspector DeKok written by Baantjer have achieved a large following among readers in the Netherlands. A television series based on these novels reaches an even wider Dutch audience. Launched nearly a decade ago, over 100 episodes of the *Baantjer* series have aired on Dutch channel RTL4.

Known as the "Dutch Conan Doyle," Baantjer's following continues to grow and conquer new territory.

DEKOK AND THE SOMBER NUDE

The gray sleuth is forced to deal with a most gruesome murder: a naked, dismembered young woman has been found in the city dump. DeKok faces death as an inevitable part of life, but when things turn this macabre, it's a hard pill to swallow.

ISBN-13: 978-1-933108-16-2

DEKOK AND THE GEESE OF DEATH

Renowned Amsterdam mystery author Baantjer brings to life Inspector DeKok in another stirring potboiler full of suspenseful twists and unusual conclusions.

ISBN-13: 978-0-9725776-6-3

DEKOK AND MURDER BY MELODY

"Death is entitled to our respect," says Inspector DeKok, who finds himself once again amidst dark dealings. A triple murder in the Amsterdam Concert Gebouw has him unveiling the truth behind two dead ex-junkies and their housekeeper.

ISBN-13: 978-0-9725776-9-4

DEKOK AND THE DEATH OF A CLOWN

A high-stakes jewel theft and a dead clown blend into a single riddle for Inspector DeKok to solve. The connection of the crimes at first eludes him.

ISBN-13: 978-1-933108-03-2

DEKOK AND VARIATIONS ON MURDER

During one of her nightly rounds, housekeeper Mrs. Van Hasbergen finds a company president dead in his boardroom. She rushes up to her apartment to call someone, but who? Deciding it better to return to the boardroom, she finds the dead man gone.

ISBN-13: 978-1-933108-04-9

DeKok and Murder by Installment
Although at first it seemed to be a case for the narcotics division, this latest investigation soon evolves into a series of sinister murders involving drug smuggling and child prostitution.
ISBN-13: 978-1-933108-07-0

DeKok and Murder on Blood Mountain
The trail of a recent crime leads Inspector DeKok to Bloedberg (Blood Mountain), Belgium, a neighborhood in Antwerp. Seems a man was fished from the Scheldt River, and DeKok has been summoned to help with the investigation.
ISBN-13: 978-1-933108-13-1

DeKok and the Dead Lovers
Inspector DeKok and his partner Vledder are ordered to protect the art treasures of a millionaire. During their watch, they are called away to help prevent the execution of a young man. That same night a priceless silver ewer is stolen from the exhibition. Although at first faced with a jigsaw puzzle of more than usual difficulty, the reader is slowly made aware of a course of events that, in passing, destroys a pipeline of child pornography to America.
ISBN-13: 978-1-933108-22-3

DeKok and the Mask of Death
A woman has disappeared without a trace from Hospital South in Amsterdam. Upon investigation, three more women seem to have disappeared in the same mysterious way. For the first time in his career, a hospital means more to DeKok than a place where wounded witnesses and criminals are interrogated.
ISBN-13: 978-1-93318-30-8

For a complete catalog of our books, please contact us at:

speck press
4690 Table Mountain Drive, Suite 100
Golden, Colorado 80403
e: books@speckpress.com
t: 800-992-2908
f: 800-726-7112
w: speckpress.com

Our books are available through your local bookseller.